TRADE UP

Why buy a job when you can start a career?

John Finan & Lisa Brandt

It's the authors' goal to introduce as many students and their families as possible to the option of pursuing a career in the skilled trades.

Book John Finan to speak to your class or group, in person or online, about the trades and their many opportunities and advantages. John has first-hand experience about a great life one can build by starting out in a skilled trade.

Media inquiries are also welcome.
For more information please visit www.tradeupbook.ca

Trade Up

ISBN 9781738804313
90000 >
9 781738 804313

THE FACTS

In January 2022, The Government of Ontario launched Skilled Trades Ontario, to improve trades training and simplify services. The new agency aims to prepare more workers for in-demand jobs in the trades.

- By 2025, one in five jobs will be in the trades.
- Over 700,000 skilled tradespeople in total are expected to retire by 2028.
- The most severe shortages are among trades critical to the coming infrastructure boom, including industrial mechanics, welders, and boilermakers.
- Women made up just 11% of new registrants for apprenticeship programs in 2019 and continue to represent less than 4% of workers in the most in-demand trades.
- Immigrants comprised 8.7% of apprentices despite accounting for more than 20% of the population.
- The COVID-19 pandemic had a significant impact on Canada's apprenticeship systems. Apprenticeship data from

2020 shows the largest year-over-year declines in new apprenticeship registrations and certifications since the data series began in 1991.

- It takes the average student fourteen years to repay student loans.
- There are more than 1.7 million student debt holders in Canada, each with an average of $26,000 in debt.
- One in six insolvencies in Canada was signed by a student debtor.
- Get a trade by 22, a degree by 27, and never have any debt.
- Getting a trade is a direct path to self-employment (if the tradesperson wishes).
- A plumber can work anywhere in the world, always.

CHAPTER ONE

Bob Turpin had been thinking about Career Day since his old high school classmate had asked him to make a presentation a few weeks earlier. Patty Martin, now Ms. Martin to her grade 11 students, had been in the same homeroom as Bob all through high school. The same school, in fact, that Bob was parking his pick-up in front of now. Bob's F-150 crew cab sported a custom metallic navy paint job, with his company's name emblazoned in white lettering across the doors on both sides: *Turpin General Contractors*. It matched the navy windbreaker he wore over his long-sleeved shirt and dark jeans.

He pulled into a spot between an older, faded red Pontiac Sunfire that had seen better days, and a gold minivan. *One kid has Mom's van for the day and the other is driving the best he can afford. Probably working after school and on weekends to pay for insurance, but at least he's got wheels. Ah, high school,* thought Bob as he killed his truck's motor and unbuckled his seat belt.

Patty Martin was surprised to discover that she had butterflies over the thought of seeing her old friend after all these years. She rearranged papers on her desk and smoothed down the front of her dress. It was just nerves. Bob had become a top contractor whom everybody in town knew. She couldn't help remembering her reaction at graduation when she and her classmates had broken off into little cliques, sharing excitement over their plans. When Bob proudly told the group that he wasn't going to university and was headed directly to an electrician's apprenticeship instead, Patty reacted with more smugness than she would now like to admit.

"Not going to university. Are your parents freaking out?" she had asked him.

Bob's answer echoed in her memory.

"I'll be making my own money instead of spending theirs. I won't end up with a mountain of student debt so, no Patty, they're not freaking out at all."

A knock on the classroom door startled Patty back to the present. Her students closed the textbooks they'd been reading and shuffled in their seats.

"Anybody home?" Bob asked with a smile.

"Come in, come in! So good to see you, Bob!"

"It's been forever!"

They gave each other a quick hug, feeling the students' watchful eyes on them.

Ms. Martin backed up a couple of steps and put her arms out toward Bob like a *Price is Right* model showing off a brand-new laundry pair.

"People, meet our final presenter on this Career Day – Mr. Bob Turpin, General Contractor. Mr. Turpin is here to share his career path with us, so I hope you'll pay close attention and come up with some great questions for him. Mr. Turpin, the floor is yours."

"Thanks, Pa — uh, Ms. Martin. Hello class. I wonder if any of you can tell me what a general contractor is?"

A few hands shot up and Bob pointed to an enthusiastic-looking young man wearing a green camo hoodie. The boy stood up.

"A general contractor is the guy who puts together the whole project when a new house is being built."

He took his seat again.

"That's very close," replied Bob. "First off, it can be a guy or a girl. Lots of women are getting into the industry. And it's more than just building houses. It's builds of almost any kind. Condo buildings, townhouses, commercial buildings, too. A general contractor gathers all the tradespeople and keeps the project moving forward. It's about scheduling, staying on budget, and — in the case of a house build —keeping it as stress-free as possible for the owners.

"Everything has to go in the right order. The concrete goes in, then the framing, windows and doors, and HVAC must be done before electrical and plumbing, and drywall. They all need to get done in their time allotment and at, or under their cost estimate. And these workers are on other jobs, so you have to plan so they get to your job without a long break in between. They need to keep working to make a living. There's a lot to it. Handling problems, keeping things moving when someone gets sick, or a piece of equipment doesn't show up, labour strikes, lumber and manufacturing shortages, or unforeseen weather problems. You juggle all of this while making sure everything gets done to code before the inspectors get there.

He continued.

"When I was your age, many of the kids in my class went straight from high school into college or university. It was sort of expected, even by the school. The Guidance Counsellor would ask *which* school you'd be going to, not *whether* you'd go. Also, some kids didn't have a choice. It was understood, their whole lives, that they would go to university. Even if they didn't know yet what they wanted to do afterward. I knew long before graduation that it just wasn't the path I wanted to take.

"And keep in mind that while I'm talking about general contracting work, "the skilled trades" includes hundreds of types of jobs. Becoming a chef or a cook is a trade. Auto body repair is a trade. Carpentry. Hairdressing. So many careers. I'm here representing one area of the skilled trades but there's a lot more you can look into if you want."

A blond girl at the back of the class raised her hand.

"Yes?"

The girl asked, "Weren't your parents upset that you weren't interested in university? I'm fairly sure mine would disown me."

Bob shook his head at the familiar question. Patty Martin blushed.

"No," he said, smiling warmly. "My parents were happy that I'd found something I wanted to do, that I had an aptitude for, and they were even happier that I'd be earning a living sooner than most of my friends."

That statement prompted a murmur among the students, some of whom reacted with "whoa," and "no way."

"But let me be clear", Bob continued. "I have nothing against a college or university education. If it's your dream to become a doctor, for example, that's the way you should go. But it's not the *only* way to build a successful, rewarding life. And there are lots of advantages to taking another route to a career, like the one I took. You can always take University courses part time while doing an apprenticeship. There's an old saying work smart not hard. My advice is do both"

"So," continued the girl, "did you go to a general contractor school or something?"

"It doesn't work like that," said a male student.

"How do you know?" she shot back.

"My Dad's a plumber, that's how."

"And I'm an electrician," countered Bob. "That's my trade. I was taken on as an apprentice and started making money right away. It wasn't a lot, mind you, but most of my friends still had years of expensive school ahead of them. When they got their degrees, they also got a big student debt. They started in the red, financially."

"In the red?" asked a student.

"In the hole," offered Bob.

The students looked at each other quizzically. Realizing they didn't know what he meant, he turned to Ms. Martin and asked, "May I use the chalkboard?"

"Be my guest," she said.

Bob walked over to the board, picked up a piece of chalk and began writing numbers on the black slate. He began with his starting salary as an apprentice and listed what he earned and what he owed.

"Mr. Turpin?" A boy in the front row asked meekly. "Do you have something we could compare your numbers to? Like how much university cost and how much those students maybe made when they graduated?"

Bob nodded. "Good call."

Ms. Martin approached the chalkboard and picked up a piece of chalk.

"We'll use my experience," she said. "But I'm ballparking my current salary."

The students let out a disappointed, "Aww," in unison, smattered with some laughter.

"And these numbers are generalities. They don't include things like summer jobs or living in residence – there are variables. But it will be close to the truth."

Bob and Patty wrote their lists side by side.

When he was done, Bob's list looked like this:

5 yr. apprenticeship – annual salary
Year one: $32,000
Year two: $40,000
Year three: $48,000
Year four: $56,000
Year five: $64,000
Journey person year 1 $80,000
Journey person year 2 $80,000
Total 7-year earnings: $400,000.
Debt: 0

Patty's list was much different, based on costs, not income, until after she finished her education.

4 yr. university (BA) $7,000 x 4 = -$28,000
Teachers' college $20,000
Education cost: $48,000
First year teaching: $78,000
Total earnings (after debt): $30,000

And then Bob tallied how much further ahead he was, financially, than his old classmate.

$370,000

The adults stood back and considered their work. The implication was obvious. Bob had begun working and earning right away. He was able to pay for his courses as he attended them. Although he started at minimum wage, he was still making money as an apprentice, on the job working toward becoming certified.

After spending thousands on university, Patty was saddled by student debt. She had a good starting salary, but she needed to start paying back her loans.

The students chatted about what they saw.

Ms. Martin put down her chalk and took her place at the front of the class with her hands clasped behind her back.

"Okay, everyone. Quiet down now. So," she said, and turned to look at Bob, "I think we all see the point you're making. You made money while you learned, and you started earning more, sooner. Is that a fair assessment?"

Bob nodded. "And, that 50-thousand dollars of student debt is what's known as being "in the red" or "in the hole." I did take on some debt eventually. I got a car loan and then mortgaged a house. There's nothing wrong with some debt if you use it right and pay it down. But I didn't start out with that big number hanging over my head."

"And" she continued, "I assume you're happy with your choice?"

"I am," he answered. "I have no regrets. I enjoyed my job, and I learned a lot about the other trades in addition to electrical. Soon, I was being asked to take on bigger and bigger projects and becoming a contractor just happened naturally. I got my contractor's license and I've never looked back. I didn't really set out to chase money, but I wanted to avoid starting my adult life feeling like I was only working to pay off my loans."

Bob addressed the kids directly once again.

"Now, like I said, some debt can be good, even necessary, like a mortgage to own your own home instead of renting one. But credit cards, and student debt, well, I see that as a hole you must spend your income digging yourself out of. Again, some of you might want a college certificate or a university degree. I'm not against that. You could take university courses after you've started working in your trade. More education is never a bad thing.

There will always be a need for good people in the trades. Right now, for every four people who retire from a trade, there's only one to replace him or her. There's more work than they can handle and that creates job security. I knew when I started my own company that even if I fell flat on my face, I could always hire on with someone else. I've been lucky, sure. . . "

Bob tapped the top of Patty's desk.

"But knock wood, I'm in a secure industry with a bright future. And I don't worry about work drying up for me or the people who work for me. You can't automate what we do."

A male student's hand shot up. "What do you drive?"

Most of the boys snickered. A man's wheels said a lot about him, especially to a teen who's just gaining his independence by learning to drive.

Bob laughed, too. "A Ford F-150 crew cab. I turn it in for a new one every year. It's a perk of needing a truck for my business. That, and writing off my gas and insurance as business expenses."

"And what do you drive, Ms. Martin?" the boy asked.

Patty bit her lip, wishing she didn't have to answer.

"A 6-year-old Pontiac Sunfire."

Bob looked at her and suppressed a smile. "Is it red?"

"Yes, it is," she said.

"You know, students," explained Bob, "it doesn't matter what you drive or how big your house is, no matter what the Kardashians try to tell you. What matters is laying your head down at night and getting a great night's sleep because you're not worried about owing a lot more money than you have and wondering how you're ever going to pay it back while still feeding your family and keeping a roof over your head. Success is waking up in the morning and looking forward to going to work because you love it. And if what you love to do doesn't require a university degree and a boatload of debt, it's worth thinking about. Don't you think?"

Bob scanned the young faces and wasn't surprised to see many of them looking skeptical. He knew that many of their parents expected them to get a university degree. Some would pursue their passion that way, sure, but many would only go to please their parents. The cost could get enormous, especially if they lived away from home. And then there were books and other must-haves. *If it wasn't what the kid wanted, why make him do it*, he thought.

Bob cleared his throat.

"Some of you haven't made up your minds about your future and that's okay. This is a great time to explore your options and consider what you might like to do. My company takes part in a program called Ride and Decide. If you're interested, we'll partner you for a couple of weeks with a journeyman in one of the trades you're curious about. You'll get to go to their jobs with them and see what it's really like. You might love it, or you might not but it's a great way to find out for sure. If any of you would like to do it or find out more about it, just come up and see me today or Ms. Martin can help you get in touch. Thanks for having me. I really enjoyed talking to you all."

The class applauded politely. Students began piling books and stuffing phones and other items into their backpacks.

Bob and Patty took the opportunity to visit and ask after each other's families. Bob was talking about his teenage daughter Corinne, and her love of painting, when he felt a presence just over his shoulder. One boy and girl had approached him and were waiting for his conversation with Ms. Martin to come to a natural end.

Ms. Martin spoke first.

"Yes, Jacob, Madison, do you have questions for Mr. Turpin?"

The kids looked at each other, wondering which one of them should go first.

"I don't really have a question," said Madison, a blonde, athletic-looking 17-year-old. "I wanted to sign up for that ride-along thingy."

"Ride and Decide," corrected Bob, gently. "Yeah, sure, we can get you on board with that. Is there one trade you're interested in? Or just general stuff?"

"I think I'd like to try electrical, like you. Everybody needs lights, right? It's not like they'll go out of style," Madison said.

"That's true. And what about you — Jacob, is it?"

Jacob hadn't put his hand up during Bob's talk, but he certainly stood out with his spiky red hair and a silver nose ring.

"Yeah," Jacob said. "I don't really know what I want to do but I'd like to find out so maybe everybody would stop asking me, you know?"

"I get that," agreed Bob.

"Well, what do you think, Bob? Can we get these two into the program?" Ms. Martin asked.

Bob couldn't hide his delight.

"For sure! You have a ride to get to and from the job sites?"

They nodded yes.

He dug around in his jacket pocket and pulled out some business cards. "Call tomorrow or Monday. Tell them you were in Ms. Martin's class and that we talked. They'll put you through to me and we'll get you in and signed up. I'll explain everything when I see you next. You'll need to have your parents' permission and I'll get you the paperwork for that. It's all online. That sound okay?"

The teens nodded shyly.

"You'll have to go shopping, too. You'll need steel-toed boots, safety goggles, and a pair of gloves. All CSA approved. Safety is job one. I'll supply hard hats. Check out the big box stores. Safety shoe stores. Poke around. You can get a good deal."

Madison and Jacob nodded that they understood.

Students from the next class began filing in and it was time for Bob to get back to work. He needed to check on the crews building a multi-million-dollar home on the outskirts of town.

CHAPTER TWO

Bob was naturally a morning person. He enjoyed getting up with the early birds, brewing the day's first cup of coffee in the stillness of his house before his family woke up and the wonderful chaos of a new day began. It was 6 am, the day after his talk at the high school. Bob lingered over his coffee and ruminated over what he'd told the class.

Had he been too hard on Patty about taking the university route? He didn't think so. The facts spoke for themselves. Her choices got her toward the career she wanted but they also saddled her with a mountain of debt that would take her several more years to pay off. Bob had also freely chosen his career, but in contrast to Patty, he'd been virtually independent since the day he left high school.

Maybe he didn't fully flesh out all the roads a person could take to get to where he was today. Bob had only mentioned trade school in passing. The courses took less time because they were more narrowly focused, had smaller class sizes, and started at various times throughout the year. He was on the job as an apprentice for four months, in school for two months, lather, rinse and repeat.

Students had the choice of signing up for college courses in the trades. That might be a way to satisfy parents who insist on at least a college certificate, but it still might result in some accumulated debt. And that route usually meant taking courses that were unrelated to the student's destination to fill out a term's worth of classes. Plus, the school year was set in stone.

Getting into a trade wasn't an easy way around a good education as some people thought, especially back when Bob was a teenager. For starters, you had to have earned a high school diploma, and decent marks certainly helped. Electrical work required a good head for math. High school students often wondered when they'd ever put algebra to practice in real life. They'd know the answer to that question if they became electricians.

Bob's apprenticeship wasn't easy, and although he never doubted he was on the right path, sometimes it felt like the 5 years would never end. There were days when he thought he would scream if someone asked him to roll out another spool of wire one more time. But he had been earning a living and learning at the same time. He had to pay for his courses, sure, but they were a darn sight less expensive than any place that offered degrees. He also had to buy his own tools, which he did a little at a time. He needed decent steel-toed boots and a few other items like a tool belt at a time when he didn't have much money to spare. But he stuck to a budget and made it work.

Before he turned 25, Bob was able to save for a down payment on a starter home. After he married Alyssa, they pooled their resources and bought a bigger house, suitable for a family. And they were able to invest in a couple of rental properties that were fully occupied and more than paying for themselves while gaining equity. He wouldn't have been able to launch such a good start in life if he'd been expected to pay back tens of thousands in student loans.

Bob finished his coffee and looked out the kitchen window at the buds on a Japanese magnolia. Soon they'd burst open and cover the tree in pink flowers. His wife loved that tree. Seeing it bloom never failed to make her happy. Bob smiled, rinsed his mug in the sink, and got ready for work.

CHAPTER THREE

The following week, the day arrived when the two students from Patty's class who were interested in Ride and Decide would be coming to prepare for their first-time job-shadowing professional tradespeople. When Bob arrived at his company's building — first one in the door, of course — he got his morning organized and responded to a few emails. It was another busy day with a half-dozen HVAC units going out to be installed in new homes under construction and various other residential jobs on the schedule.

Jacob was a clean slate who didn't know which trade might suit him best. Bob decided to send him out with a residential HVAC installation team. They were highly experienced and made it look easy, but Bob could imagine Jacob's head swimming with project details later in the day. Jacob's number one task would be to avoid getting in the team's way.

As for Madison, if electrical was what she wanted to learn, Bob would pair her up with Jordan Lattan, an excellent electrician. Jordan had been with the company for about 7 years and was still young enough to be able to relate to a high school student. However, Jordan also had a family of his own and a growing portfolio of rental properties. He was on his way to becoming a bit of a land baron. He was also meticulous about safety and leaving a customer's home as clean as he found it. Bob felt good about the example Jordan would set for Madison. He'd let Jordan know he'd have company on the job for a while.

Bob tried not to put expectations on the students' experiences, but he did hope they'd find it worth their while. They might love the work, or they might not. That wasn't for him to guess. Besides, he knew little about these kids and what they were capable of. Would they glove up and lend a hand when asked? Or would they balk when called up to check something in a spider-filled, dusty basement? He had no idea. He would simply have to wait for it to unfold.

Mid-afternoon, Bob's phone buzzed as he was preparing to leave company headquarters to check in on a build. The students, Madison, and Jacob were at reception. They'd arrived together, which was something Bob didn't expect. Later he'd learn that Jacob had his own car and had offered Madison a ride. Bob asked the receptionist to show them to his office.

Their young faces peered in through the open doorway and Bob motioned for them to enter.

They were both dressed casually in jeans, T-shirts, and hoodies. Good start. Other kids had arrived at job sites in high heels and dress pants. That would never do. They were sent home to dress down before returning.

Madison held onto the straps of a blue backpack. Jacob stuffed his hands in his hoodie pockets and tried to appear comfortable, but he was clearly anxious.

"Madison and Jacob, right? Glad you both made it down today."

"Thanks, Mr. T.," said Jacob, oblivious to *The A-Team* reference that was not lost on a man of Bob's age. He wanted to say, "call me Bob," but he knew from experience that keeping things more formal was a better idea, for now at least. He'd see how their job shadowing went before deciding whether to get chummy with them. "Mr. T." was about as casual as he'd let them get.

"So," Bob wondered, "you have your consent forms printed from the web?"

Madison, who had yet to say anything, dropped her backpack and rummaged through it until she found a folded piece of paper. Jacob pulled his crumpled form out of a back pocket. Both teens presented the papers warily. Bob looked them over and nodded.

"Looks good. So, tell me, what do your parents think about you doing this?"

Madison shrugged. "They're okay with it, I guess. They think it's going to be hard work and I might not like it."

"It *is* going to bc hard work," Bob said, "and I guess we'll find out whether you like it or not. That's kind of the point, right? Jacob? What about your folks?"

Jacob looked at his feet and kicked non-existent rocks on the carpet. "They're happy I'm looking into something. I think my Mom and Stepdad are afraid I'll live in their basement for the rest of my life." He looked up and smiled.

"Some people decide on their futures a little later. Some do it a bit at a time," explained Bob. "So, are you ready?"

The students nodded in the affirmative.

"Great," said Bob with a wide grin. "I don't have a big speech for you. Just be alert. Staying safe is the top priority and our guys are good about watching out for hazards, but you're also responsible for yourselves. So, if something concerns you or you don't want to do it because you're unsure, ask questions, tell them you need them to explain it again — don't do anything you don't completely understand, okay? Madison, you'll be around live wires and I don't have to tell you how dangerous that can be if you make a mistake. Jacob, watch your head! You can bang your noggin on a hundred different things on these jobs. You'll get hard hats on your way out. You're expected to wear the hats. Understood?"

"Yes, sir," said Madison. Jacob nodded.

They're not saying much, thought Bob. *They're not acting overconfident. That's a good sign. Know-it-alls are hard to train. A good job-shadowing experience involves listening well and following instructions.*

Bob exited his office and the students followed. It was time for them to meet their mentors.

CHAPTER FOUR

Madison had only been on the worksite for an hour, but she was ready for their scheduled break. She was also excited about what she'd seen so far. Mr. Lattan worked fast, though Madison had nothing to compare it to, he took the time to explain everything he did and why it was done that way. The new build they were on was in its end stages. Plumbing and HVAC were in, drywall was up, and the office building was getting close to having its new tenants move in. Madison wanted to know more about what it took to install the electrical system before she came on the scene.

"We're here from the start, pretty much, putting in conduits and wiring the place as they're laying concrete and building the structure. Most of our work no one ever sees again once it's sealed up. But we have the satisfaction of knowing it's in there and working as it ought to."

"Is this what it's like every day?" Madison asked.

Jordan shook his head as he tossed another potato chip in his mouth.

"Not at all. Every day is different. You might be working with new people or doing an industrial or residential job. I can drive around the city and point to all the buildings and houses I've worked on. It's . . . satisfying."

"And Mr. Turpin thinks there will always be work."

"He's right," Jordan agreed, "because there's such a shortage of electricians. I don't get it, really. It's steady work and the pay is good. Better than I'd get anywhere else right out of high school, and I can work anywhere. My wife is talking about wanting to move back east to be closer to her family. I'd have no trouble getting a good job if we decide to go."[1]

Madison took another bite of the energy bar her Mom made her put in her backpack. She was grateful for it and the bottle of water her Mom also insisted she takes with her.

"Have you ever been electrocuted?" she asked.

Jordan snorted a surprised laugh. "I think you mean shocked. Yes, I have been shocked but that was a long time ago. Electricity and I have mutual respect for each other. I handle it properly and it doesn't kill me."

Jordan thought for a moment before continuing.

"Working with live power seems more dangerous if you don't know what you're doing. It is dangerous, but that's why you need to really pay attention to things like when we shut the power off and on, you know? It's good that you listen more than you talk. But don't be afraid to ask questions."

"I don't know enough to know what to ask," said Madison.

"You will," Jordan said. "It's only day one. It's all probably a little confusing."

Madison nodded and took a long draw on her bottle of water.

---

[1] Ontario Investing in Construction Sector to Combat Labour Shortage. https://news.ontario.ca/en/release/1002367/ontario-investing-in-construction-sector-to-combat-labour-shortage

"What do you think so far?" Jordan asked.

"I love it!" Madison exclaimed. "I think I could see myself doing this. Unless there's something really awful, I haven't seen yet. Like you said, it's just the first day."

"Oh, don't worry. They don't send us into live snake pits anymore like they did in medieval times!"

"Medieval electricians, eh?"

"Oh yeah. Hard work back then. Getting over moats and scaling castle walls. Nothing like it is today."

"And the dragons," said Madison. "You must have had a tough time with them."

They both laughed.

Madison turned serious. "Have you ever thought about going out on your own? Starting your own company?"

"I have but there's a lot more to it than just registering a company, you know. There's advertising and bookkeeping and all of that. And I'd have to compete with Mr. Turpin's shop and others like it. They have a huge head start and a good reputation. Plus, the hours would be longer, at the start, anyway. I like my 9-to-5 life and so does my family. I'm home for dinner every night and to read my kids their bedtime stories."

They chewed in silence for a couple of minutes, then Jordan spoke again.

"Something else when it comes to my family. Medical and dental coverage. It would be so expensive to pay for it on my own. Do you know what it costs to take a kid to the dentist?"

Madison said, "I don't really know how much it costs. Is it a lot?"

Jordan nodded.

"If you need a prescription and have to pay out of pocket, too, that can be pricey. Money is a big part of it, but there's more to it. I like working with a team sometimes, as well as on my own. I wouldn't get to do that if I were my own boss. It's just not for me, I guess."

"Makes sense," said Madison, "but it's nice to know it's an option."

"For sure," Jordan replied.

They finished their snacks, crumpled their wrappers, and tucked them away. It was time to get back to work.

CHAPTER FIVE

Jacob leaned on his shovel and took a few deep breaths. The HVAC team stood back and watched with bemused expressions on their faces. Kevin and Tim had been partners for a long time. Kevin, the more experienced of the two, was in his fifties and a fitness fanatic. He went for a 5k run every morning before work, and at night worked out with free weights. He was tall, with broad shoulders, and wore his head shaved.

Tim was in his thirties, shorter and more compact. He was particular about how things were done. Neither man would cut corners, but Tim was the fussier of the two. His favourite pastime was taking his two young sons fishing for pike way up north. He loved camping and almost anything to do with being outdoors.

It was Saturday morning around 7:30, Jacob's third day on the job with the two men. A central air condenser unit for the customer, Ms. Barker, was unboxed and ready for installation. The guys had brought the piece over on a hand cart. It weighed several hundred pounds, mostly because of the density of the copper coil inside.

Kevin expected the job to be straightforward because the new unit was a replacement for a 15-year-old system that was about to fail. The existing ductwork was sufficient for the new system although it had a greater cooling ability. No retrofitting was necessary. Ms. Barker would feel the difference, going from 20,000 to 36,000 BTUs.

Kevin and Tim had removed the refrigerant from the old condenser unit, disconnected the lines and carried it to the truck bed for later disposal.

Jacob had told the guys that the earlier spring he and his dad had put down a patio stone walkway to their house. That was all the evidence Tim and Kevin needed to step aside and let the teen have a go at levelling the ground for a patio stone to set the condenser unit on. They had already measured a plot of garden on the east side of the house, 12 inches from the wall. This location would limit the amount of sun on the unit to prevent it from overheating. It would also be away from tree leaves and other debris that could blow inside to the fan.

Jacob removed sticks and small rocks from the patch of earth, dug down a few inches and scraped away the soil to make it an even surface. Sweat poured down the sides of his face beneath his hard hat but he didn't dare take it off. He knew wearing it was part of the protocol. His T-shirt was soaking with sweat and clung to his back. He had already shucked off his hoodie. He tamped the soft earth with the soles of his work boots while Kevin stood watch, holding an old-fashioned aluminum level.

With the earth now straight, Jacob dipped the end of the spade into a bag of sand Kevin had brought to the house from the back of the company pickup. Jacob spread the sand on top of the dirt. He repeated this action several times until a layer of sand coated the soil underneath it. He walked back and forth on the sand and compacted it with tight steps.

The moment of truth had come. Would the ground now be even enough to place a huge, square patio stone and then the A/C unit on top and be stable? Jacob hoped his first task with these seasoned professionals would end in victory, not defeat.

"All right let's check your work," said Kevin as he approached Jacob's patch of sanded earth and held out the level. He crouched, placed the tool on the ground, and waited for the bubble to settle. Kevin put his hand over the bubble. Jacob bit his lip. Kevin looked up and smiled at him. Tim shook his head and laughed.

"You're torturing the kid," Tim said.

"No," said Kevin, and pulled his hand away from the level. "First thing you need to know is, it's never going to be perfect the first time. Dig a little out of this end and that ought to do it."

Jacob scraped some sand from one end and tamped it down at the other.

This time the read on the level was perfect. Kevin lifted and set the level down in several directions on the patch. The ground was completely straight.

Jacob blew out a huge sigh.

"Nice job, kid," said Kevin. Tim patted him on the back. Jacob grinned widely, relief showing on his sweaty face.

"Now," said Kevin, "let's see how you carry a patio stone!"

With the stone set and the condenser unit in place with no signs of a wobble, it was time to head to the basement. Jacob watched the men replace the air handler — they called it a blower — with one that had a greater capacity to match the new, higher-efficiency condenser unit outside. They connected the mains and checked everything over twice to make sure it was all working properly. The job took a couple of hours.

Once the unit was running perfectly, the men gathered up their tools and packed everything away neatly in the pickup bed.

"Hey kid," said Kevin, opening the passenger door, "now we get Ms. Barker to sign off on the job. Let me show you how it works. You just hold out this gizmo," he said, pulling an electronic device the size of a label maker from the truck console. "She signs her name with this pen on the side. It just says that we did the job we said we did. Then you press print, and her copy comes out. The information automatically goes back to the office and gets uploaded to the computer. And then we're done. Shall we?"

They walked to Ms. Barker's front landing and Kevin rang the doorbell. When Ms. Barker appeared, they explained what they had done and that they needed her signature. She complied and thanked them for, "making my house livable again." She put out her hand and shook with Kevin and Tim but suddenly grabbed Jacob into a tight hug.

"You've made an old woman so happy," she said. "And on a Saturday, too. Thank you, young man!"

Jacob's face turned beet red, and he managed to mutter, "You're welcome, ma'am."

On their way back to the pickup, Tim said, "Isn't that a great way to end the workday? We made a customer happy, and you, my young friend, even got hugged. It doesn't get much better than that."

"It's only 10:15," said Jacob, "what do we do until noon?"

"We go buy ourselves a fresh cup of coffee. Or an ice-cold beverage. Whatever you want, kid," Kevin said.

"Isn't this supposed to be an 8-hour day," Jacob asked.

"Six hours on Saturday," said Kevin.

"I don't get the math. How does a 6-hour day, work into a 40-hour week?"

"We alternate Saturdays," said Tim. "So, everyone gets a shot at one shorter day that week. We didn't work Monday, see? So, we did four eight-hour days and then today. Next week, it's back to Monday to Friday and someone else has Monday off and works next Saturday. It's a nice change. A long weekend every few weeks."

Kevin picked up the explanation.

"Maybe Monday's job will take us until 6 or 7 at night. Last week I had to go to houses at opposite ends of town to write up estimates and that took me 'til well after 6. And then a shorter day like this one makes up for it. It all tends to work out in the end. Really, we work a 40-hour week, but not always an 8 or 6-hour day."

"And you're okay with that?" Jacob asked.

"Sure," said Tim. "It's not always like today, of course, but it's nice when it is."

They climbed into the truck, Kevin driving, Tim in the passenger seat and Jacob in the back seat of the crew cab. They pulled out of the customer's driveway and headed into town.

Jacob leaned forward. "So, why did you get into this job?"

"Well kiddo, I was seriously thinking about becoming a lawyer," said Kevin.

"Are you kidding me?" asked Tim.

"Nope. Seriously. It was the first thing I thought I'd like to do. I had the grades. Loved school. Then I found out the reality of it. Three or four years of university, minimum, then articling, which is like an apprenticeship for lawyers. Then you must pass the bar exam. It's expensive and takes so long. When you're all done, you're working your way up a ladder with thousands of other young legal eagles while still paying for school. And the hours. Talk about staying at work until the job is done! By the time you get to the fun part in the courtroom, it's been weeks of late nights and researching cases. Nah. I have set hours here. And if I work overtime, I get paid overtime. And that lady's smile just now? That's as good as winning a case every time."

"What about you, Tim?"

"Same," said Tim, with a deadpan look on his face.

Kevin laughed hard.

"No, not really," said Tim. "I knew I wanted to do something with my hands. Build or make something. Figuring out where ductwork should go and putting it in, or diagnosing an intermittent problem with a furnace is close enough. At the end of the day, you've put something together that changes someone's life for the better. It's a good feeling. And it pays well too."

Jacob thought about that for a moment and then asked, "But isn't the pay pretty bad when you start?"

"It sure is," laughed Tim. "Minimum wage, most places. But let me ask you this. How much do you get paid when you're in university or college?"

Jacob nodded. "Nothing."

"Right," agreed Tim. "You're paying out the whole time. And yeah, it's not great money when you're an apprentice but it gets better quickly. They want to make sure it's what you want, that you'll stick with it. And then when you're licensed, it's like you suddenly won the lottery."

"It's true," said Kevin. "I was living at home with my folks, paying some rent, but not much. I planned it out when I apprenticed and lived within my means. I could still go out with my buddies on the weekends and afford to have a good time. Their jobs were paying the same, but they weren't on a path like I was. I'm not putting their choices down. I just took a different road. The next year I made a little more. Then a little more. I have no complaints."

"That's right," said Tim. "And now we're up to . . . "

Both men put their pinkie nails in their teeth like Mike Myers' Dr. Evil and said, "One billion dollars!"

They all laughed.

"That's great," said Jacob, settling back into the seat. "That means the coffee's on you!"

CHAPTER SIX

Madison enjoyed job shadowing Jordan even more than she thought she would. Jordan was patient and encouraging. He hadn't let her get into harm's way, but he had allowed her to help with some of the smaller tasks, like cutting wire and screwing in wall plates. Madison wasn't in a rush. She saw the satisfaction Jordan got out of getting everything done right.

As far as she could tell, being an electrician was fifty percent electrical work, 25 percent problem-solving and 25 percent customer relations. An electrician really needed to have the right personality to be successful in the job. She wondered whether she had that type of personality. She thought she might.

Breaks had turned into Q&A sessions, with Madison barely able to wait until she could start peppering Jordan with questions.

"What's the worst job you ever had to do?"

Jordan chewed on his sandwich and looked off in the distance to consider this.

"It had to be the cat lady."

"Cat lady?" Madison asked.

"Yeah," said Jordan. "It was a lady who lost power in half her house. Turned out it was mice chewing on wires. But she had a bunch of cats and, well, she wasn't too fussy about keeping their litter boxes clean. I nearly gagged going in there. The job itself was all right. But the cats — brrrrrrr."

"Let me guess, you're a dog person?"

"After that day, I was!" Jordan laughed.

"Okay, what about the most dangerous job?"

"That's an easy one. We got a call because a woman got a shock when she hammered a nail in a wall to hang a picture. Pretty random, right? Well, we ended up having to remove drywall in that spot to figure it out. Turns out the previous owner had hired someone, or maybe he did it himself, but they clearly had no idea what they were doing. He used pieces of wire that weren't long enough, so he stripped the insulation and twisted the copper together. And the nail had just touched the edge of a bare wire. Another couple of millimetres to the left and that would be one very shocked lady."

"Wow, really? It was that close?"

"Oh yeah," said Jordan. "And it wasn't the only place in the house with those short, bare wires behind drywall. It was a huge house, like, five bedrooms, four floors. The place was a fire trap. I felt so bad for the new homeowner because she'd had the house checked out by a home inspector, but they don't find this kind of thing. It's just lucky she wasn't hurt. She had called me, and I was duty-bound to report it. We ended up making holes in all the walls. Rewiring everything. It was a nightmare. But she wouldn't have been able to insure her home unless it was all fixed and brought up to code. It was crazy."

"Why would anyone do that? Why not do it right?"

Jordan rubbed a forefinger and thumb together.

“Money. That’s the beginning and end of it. They’re being cheap. There’s a reason you’re supposed to use a licensed electrician and get permits and have the work inspected by an electrical inspector before it’s closed. This person, whoever they were, just went ahead and did what they did, patched it up, and if the lights worked, they didn’t care that it wasn’t to code. A little knowledge is a dangerous thing. Pair it with a customer who’s so cheap they’re willing to put their family in danger, well, what can I tell you?”

“Wow.”

“Agreed,” said Jordan. “Okay, that breaker panel isn’t going to replace itself. Let’s get at it.”

CHAPTER SEVEN

In his two weeks with the HVAC team, Jacob felt he'd learned as much as he needed to know about the trade. Kevin and Tim had allowed him to connect ductwork after they'd planned it, and afterward, they thoroughly checked his work. They showed him the ways various machines functioned. It was great to have learned so much, but Jacob didn't think it was the right vocation for him. Although Kevin and Tim said every day was different, Jacob felt there wasn't enough variety in the day-to-day routine to keep him interested. He appreciated the way Tim and Kevin treated him like one of the guys, but he was ready to explore something else.

He decided to give carpentry a try.

Jacob's grandfather made wooden birdhouses as a hobby. He sold a few here and there but it was mostly something he did to keep busy after retirement. He had given Jacob's family at least a half dozen colourful birdhouses of various sizes. More than they could hope to put up on their small lot. Only Jacob seemed impressed with his grandpa's work. Jacob admired the way he joined the wood corners and left no gaps in the seams. Grandpa experimented with his biscuit joiner, overkill for a birdhouse, but Jacob thought it was cool. It was obvious that his grandfather took his time and made sure every project was as close to perfect as he could make it. And once he started thinking about learning a trade, Jacob thought he might be more suited to carpentry.

Jacob didn't really care much about making houses for birds, but he did like the smell and feel of the wood and admired his grandfather's dedication to quality. He had made an appointment with Mr. Turpin to talk about changing his focus.

"So, you want to look into carpentry, eh?" Bob Turpin said.

"I'd like to try it."

"Sure. HVAC's not for you?"

"I don't think so. But I appreciate learning about it. I feel like I understand how HVAC works now. Basically, anyway."

"You'll never forget what you learned on this job. I guarantee it."

"Kevin and Tim were great. They make a good team."

"One of our best," admitted Bob. "They didn't play any practical jokes on you, did they?"

"No," said Jacob, "they were just fun to be around."

"Attitude. Remember I mentioned that a long time ago? A good attitude makes a world of difference."

Jacob nodded in agreement.

"Okay then," Bob said, "this is what Ride and Decide is all about. You took HVAC for a spin, and it wasn't your thing. Now, you probably haven't noticed any carpenters around here. But I can hook you up with a company I've worked with on a lot of jobs. They do frames and finishing, mostly. You'll get a good taste for it."

"Sounds good," said Jacob, "and thanks."

"You're welcome, Jacob. Let me make a quick call. If you hang around for a few minutes, I'll have an idea of whether or not this will work out."

Jacob wandered down the tiled hallway into the break room. It was typical for a mid-size company, with a coffee maker, a microwave, a fridge, and a couple of tables with plastic chairs. A quiet place to get a beverage or eat lunch.

Jacob passed the time waiting for Bob by reading postings on the bulletin board. Someone was selling their tools because they'd recently upgraded to a more expensive set. Another note was a plea for a reliable babysitter. There was a notice about a staff BBQ coming up in a couple of weeks. And black marker scrawled on white paper appealed for players to take part in an upcoming softball tournament for charity. Jacob pulled one of the tabs off the bottom of the sheet. He hadn't played ball since elementary school, but the note gave him a feeling of team spirit. He didn't want Turpin Contractors to forfeit to a rival because they were a player short.

Bob entered the break room with a yellow notepad in his hand.

"Okay, Jacob, you're good to go. You start next week, same schedule as here, after school, until about six. Here's the address and the name of your contact. You'll need to download the consent form again and have a parent sign it and turn in our hard hat. They'll give you one of theirs."

Bob looked at Jacob's sneakers and his jaw nearly hit the floor.

"You've been wearing those on the job?"

"No sir," said Jacob, "I left my boots in my car. They're a little dirty for walking around the office."

"Whew," said Bob with relief. "Okay, if you can get a decent pair of gloves, great. If not, I'm sure they'll have some kicking around the site. You belong to Top Quality Carpentry now, Jacob. Best of luck."

Bob held out his hand and Jacob shook with a firm grip and a wide smile. He supposed he wouldn't need to resurrect his baseball skills on behalf of Turpin Contractors after all. He was moving on.

CHAPTER EIGHT

Bob and his wife, Alyssa had date nights on Fridays. This Friday night was a double date at the home of their neighbours and close friends, Barry, and Alison Fletcher. Barry managed a bank branch and Alison ran an eCommerce business out of their home. Like the Turpins, the Fletchers had teenage children and busy lives.

Bob and Barry sat on Muskoka chairs on the back deck of the Fletchers' huge mid-century modern home. Steaks sizzled slowly on the BBQ under Barry's watchful eye. Talk turned, as it often did, to work.

"Interest rates are so low," said Barry, "and we're signing off on home lines of credit like crazy. But you know what people are finding? They can't book a contractor or renovator to save their life. They have the money but there's no one available to do the work."[2]

Bob nodded. "I saw this coming years ago. It's incredible how much available work there is and how few people there are to do it. I've been thinking about starting a home renovation team

---

[2] Labour Shortage Trends in Canada report shows employment to job ratio at a historical low. https://www.statcan.gc.ca/en/subjects-start/labour_/labour-shortage-trends-canada

out of my shop. I know I could keep them busy. But is it worth it compared to having them working on new construction? That's my dilemma."

"You could name your price," said Barry.

"Yeah, but that doesn't seem right. Money isn't everything."

"You're saying that to a banker?" Barry laughed.

"I have room for more apprentices. We have to stick to a one-to-one ratio with our journeymen. Right now, we've got about a one-to-nine or ten. We have a couple of kids doing the Ride and Decide. But one of them is moving on. It's not an easy sector to grow."

"Yeah," agreed Barry. "And there's Mr. and Ms. Homeowner, frustrated, with 75k in a line of credit just dying to spend it and no one to take it. It's a weird situation."

"One for four," explained Bob. "One new tradesperson coming in for every four who leave. It's a real shame. We do everything within reason to hang onto the people we've got. Good workers are hard to find. And getting harder all the time."

Barry flipped the steaks. The smoke wafted past Bob and it smelled delicious.

"So, what's the solution?"

Bob leaned back and closed his eyes.

"Promote the trades better. Not just the schools or the courses, but the life you can make for yourself as a tradesperson. Money in your pocket. Health coverage for you and your family. A pension plan. Portability. And the freedom to chuck all that and hang out your own shingle and work for yourself if that's what you want. And you don't have to carry tools for your whole career. If you're good, you'll get promoted to supervisor. Change courses. There are a lot of options."

Bob sat up and became animated as he continued. His passion for the subject was apparent.

"That's the part that's missing from looking at the trades as a practical career option. Plenty of parents are still hell-bent on sending their kids to university no matter what. My girls know they can do what they want and if that's going to university, fine. But if it's something less traditional, less conventional, less … expensive … that's fine too. I think that cycle needs to get broken if we're ever going to help Mr. and Mrs. Homeowner get a new bathroom put in their basement."

"On the upside, they'll still have to pay interest on that line of credit they took out, even as low as the rates are now," Barry said with a smile, showing Bob he was only half-serious.

"You're the cliché of a heartless banker, my friend," Bob teased.

"Guilty as charged. And on that note, the steaks are done, and we can eat," said Barry, loading the meat onto a plate.

CHAPTER NINE

The condo build was easy to find. Jacob followed the construction signs until he got to the flag person who was stopping traffic every so often to allow machinery and trucks to enter and exit the site. Jacob parked near a Top-Quality Carpentry van and took in the scene.

This huge lot once belonged to one of the last remaining farmhouses within city limits. No one had farmed there for decades, and the home had fallen into disrepair, eventually abandoned over unpaid taxes. A developer snapped it up and then waited six long years before the city finally approved his plans to erect a mixed-use tower of condominiums above retail stores. The condos were already sold out based on roomy floor plans and the builder's good reputation.

The poured concrete foundation had been laid and framing was underway. This was where Jacob hoped to get a taste of the carpenter's life.

He locked his car, pulled on his hard hat and gloves, and as he walked toward the building, he scanned the site for someone in a white hard hat — the site supervisor. Jacob spotted the man away from the heart of the action, looking at a tablet. Jacob was nervous, but it wasn't as bad as when he started at Turpin's on HVAC. He knew a little more about what to expect on a job site and that knowledge gave him confidence. This site was much bigger than anything he'd ever attended before. Noisier too, with nail guns, hammers, and other tools sounding off in a symphony of percussion.

"Excuse me, sir," Jacob said. "I'm Jacob Lee. Mr. Turpin sent me."

The site manager looked up with a pained expression. Clearly, he had been concentrating on the tablet and an interruption wasn't welcome.

"Jacob who? You're one of Bob Turpin's guys?"

"No, no," Jacob said. "I'm here to work with the carpenters."

"Oh. The guy you want is over there." He pointed to a man wearing a blue hard hat and went back to studying the tablet.

Jacob approached the man wearing a blue hard hat. He was gesturing with both arms while in a heated conversation with a man in a yellow hat. As he got closer, Jacob picked up on the argument.

"I don't care if you have to carry it on your head! I want that lumber here and I want it now. Stacked. Ready! Like I told you yesterday and the day before!"

"Yes sir," said yellow hat meekly.

"Damn it!" said blue hat as he clamped his hands on his hips and turned his back to the departing yellow hat just in time to see Jacob step beside him.

"Dude!" he yelled, startled.

"Jacob, sir." Jacob stuck out his hand. "Mr. Turpin sent me."

"Right. Mike Burgess," the blue hat said, and shook. "Well, welcome aboard Jacob. We're going to get you into framing, eh? You've got the hard hat, gloves and . . ." he paused to look at Jacob's feet, "decent steel-toed boots. I'd say you're good to go. You ever framed a building before?"

"No, sir," replied Jacob honestly.

"Just do what you're told and if you're told to stay out of the way, do that. See those guys over there?"

Jacob nodded.

"Every one of them is your boss now. They're all journeymen and they haven't had an apprentice underfoot in quite a while, so don't mind them if they're a little bit gruff. There's no handholding here. You're probably going to get yelled at for no good reason at least once or twice. We're all trying to get the job done on time and on budget, y'hear?"

"Okay," Jacob said.

"What are you waiting for? Get over there and help them lift that wall. No time like the present, son."

Jacob broke into a trot and aimed for a wall stud between two of the guys. They barely noticed him under the strain of lifting the wall into place. Someone yelled "hold up" while another man held a level vertically against an end.

"It's good!" he shouted, and a couple more guys standing by with nail guns, rushed in to secure the wall into place.

Gradually, the men let go of the structure and took a few steps back.

"Mitch," said one of the blue hats, and thrust out his hand at Jacob.

"Jacob. Intern, I guess," Jacob said as they shook.

Mitch said, "Just keep showing up where you're needed like that, and you'll do fine. We've got lots of guys but there's never enough of us."

"Will do," Jacob said, as he put his hands on his hips and waited to see what he'd be needed for next.

CHAPTER TEN

Bob was enjoying a quiet day at the office. Quiet days made him happy because they meant everything was going along as it should. No one calling in a panic because of a crisis. Everyone handling their responsibilities. Bob hired good people and let them do their jobs. They only called him when something unusual needed to be handled and they needed a higher authority to make decisions.

He was sifting through emails. They were mostly the usual fare. Inquiries from potential vendors, offers to clean his ducts, and dreaded spam. As he scrolled down the list, one email caught his attention with the subject line, *Teaching?* The return address was a local college. He clicked on the email.

> SUBJECT: Teaching?
> FROM: Jane Witherall, Human Resources
>
> Dear Mr. Turpin,
>
> We have an opening in the Construction Project Management program and your name was sent to me as a potential candidate.

The position is part-time, and we'd be willing to plan the classes around your schedule.

Do you have any interest in teaching?

There would be little, if any, research necessary. Your daily experiences on the job as the head of your own company will suffice. We can supply you with any regulatory material you might need.

Please let us know at your earliest convenience and we will arrange a meeting.

Thank you.

Sincerely,

Ms. Jane Witherall

Bob was intrigued. He hadn't given much thought to teaching other than as an abstract concept. It was something he tucked away in the back of his mind to consider "someday." Well, it looked like someday was here.

It had been about ten years since Bob had picked up tools other than on occasion. That was always the plan. He'd become a journeyman and work his way into general contracting. He had liked electrical work, but he also liked management and had an affinity for it. Was teaching the logical next step? Could it be something to toss into the mix of a diversified career?

He supposed the first step was to respond to the email and find out.

Dear Ms. Witherall,

Thank you for your email. I'm intrigued by the idea of teaching at the college level.

I'd like to take you up on your offer to get together and discuss it further. Please let me know when you'd like to do that. My days are flexible.

Regards,

Bob Turpin

CHAPTER ELEVEN

Madison sat cross-legged on her bed, leaning on a hill made of throw pillows against a tufted linen headboard, flipping through the latest issue of *Mother Earth News*. A headline on the front that teased an article about renewable energy caught her eye. Becoming an electrician didn't have to mean just wiring houses and buildings, although she found that stuff interesting enough. Madison knew that these special skills were needed to make everything from wind turbines to solar arrays operational. Becoming an electrician wasn't just a great career choice today, it had endless possibilities for the future. The thought of working in the green energy sector excited her and she wanted to learn all she could about it.

She was concentrating so hard that she didn't notice her mom enter her bedroom.

"You know, Mads," said her mother, making Madison's whole body react in a startled twitch, "I never have to worry about you when you spend your free time reading *Mother Earth News*."

Madison smiled warmly at her mom.

"I'm just getting some information on renewable energy. I don't know much about it, but I think I want to be a part of it."

"As an electrician," her mother asked but it came out as a statement.

"As an electrician," Madison confirmed.

Her Mom sat on the side of Madison's bed.

"You really want to do this, huh? I haven't seen you this focused on something since Beyonce came to town when you were 13!"

"Mom!"

"It's true! You've changed your mind about what you want to do a hundred times. You're young, you could get an English degree and then do something completely different, but you'll have the degree in your back pocket if you need it. You know your father and I would help you with that, financially."

"I know," Madison said. "But if it isn't what I really want, wouldn't that be a waste of money? What if becoming an electrician is what I'm meant to do? I really like it, Mom."

"Oh, honey," said her mom sweetly. "I don't think anybody's meant to become an electrician. It's just something that some people end up doing."

Madison's eyes widened and she looked at her mother with incredulity. She could not believe what she'd just heard. She counted to five in her head, so she didn't say something she'd regret. That was a trick her mother had taught her.

"Mother! Do you really think that? Do you think that all the people who work in the trades have just given up on something better? That's so insulting. And elitist. Just who would you call if there was a problem with our electrical system? They have knowledge that you and Dad don't. They're educated, trained professionals who have a great life and make great money!"

"I'm sure you're mistaken about that, sweetie," her mom said softly.

"No, I'm not," Madison said firmly. "Journeymen electricians can easily make in the high five figures and beyond.[3] They get satisfaction from their work. They like helping people and fixing things. How could you have such a negative attitude about somebody who can do what you haven't got a clue about? That fact alone means they deserve our respect."

The women sat in silence for several minutes, neither one wanting to back down or break the stalemate.

"Mom," said Madison, finally. "Do you know where they store electricity?"

Her mother shrugged. "I guess in power plants."

"No. They don't. It can't be stored; it can only be produced. See, I'm learning these things including how and when it's dangerous and that it flows at the speed of light and that electricity is, literally, everywhere. It's an education as important as any other. And more practical than a literature degree, for me.

"Electricians will always have work. Don't you want me to have some security in the future? I could be part of saving the planet by working on green energy projects. It's a lot more than flicking switches and screwing in switch plates. I think it's cool."

Madison's Mom smiled sadly.

"I'm sorry, honey. I have always thought of certain jobs as being, you know. . . ."

"Cop outs," Madison said, finishing her mom's sentence. "I know how you've felt, Mom. You haven't exactly kept it a secret. But if I'm going to do this, I need to know that you get it. That

---

3 Job Bank Canada wages, electrician in Canada. https://www.jobbank.gc.ca/marketreport/wages-occupation/20684/ca

you're on Team Madison. I'm not taking an easy way out. There's math involved and all sorts of stuff I don't even know about yet. I want you to be happy for me. Proud of me."

"Oh Mads, I'm always proud of you."

"I want you to be proud when you tell your friends what I do. I could build robots, Mom. I could do a million things with this knowledge and keep learning forever. It's never going to be boring. It's challenging and exciting and it makes me feel excited for the future. I wish you were excited for me."

The women looked at each other for a long moment. Madison had heard the way her mom talked about tradespeople. Sure, it was great to have someone to call when they wanted flooring installed or a leak stopped in the bathroom. But she had never seen these lines of work as practical options for her own daughter.

Finally, Madison's mom said, "Well, there is more to this career than I thought, I'll give you that. Maybe I should do a little learning of my own."

She lunged across the bed and laughingly swiped *Mother Earth News* out of Madison's hand. She rolled the magazine, got off the bed and headed for the door. "Excuse me," said Madison's mother, "I have some reading to do." She winked at her daughter who smiled back.

CHAPTER TWELVE

Jacob was utterly exhausted. He thought about how little his appreciation for his grandfather's birdhouses had to do with the past few days as a carpenter's helper on a condo build. His arms ached from keeping them over his head while he helped hold up stud walls. His feet hurt from the extra weight of hauling heavy lengths of lumber from the delivery trucks to pile at the site. And his brain hurt from remembering so many pieces of information thrown at him in quick succession. Wall height, the distance between studs, the thickness of wood, all the things an inspector would check and had better not find wanting if the project was to stay on schedule.

His favourite part of the experience so far was the fast *THUK* sound of the nail gun. Using one of the tools was a different story. His coworkers made it look so easy but when it came time for Jacob to nail some boards together, he was embarrassed by his lack of good aim. He knocked small splinters off the edge of one of the 2 by 6s and one of the guys said, 'Thanks for making toothpicks." The others laughed and Jacob's face turned cherry-coloured. But he kept at it and by the end of the day, his technique had improved. He still wasn't as fast as the journeymen, but no one expected that of him. No one except Jacob, that is.

He knew he was hard on himself and expected perfection without practice, but he also wondered whether he still hadn't quite found the vocation he was looking for. He thought he was getting closer, though. But besides being a long way from birdhouses, Jacob admitted to himself that he wasn't excited about working outside with noisy, chaotic teams of men, like ants working on different parts of a hill.

Summers were hot, winters were cold, and he was more of an indoors kind of guy. He sunburned easily and in cold weather, it seemed the ends of his fingers and toes would not stay warm no matter how many layers he pulled over them. As a child, he was dragged along on family camping trips. His stepdad, Derek, who married his Mom when Jacob was 3, tried in vain to start a tradition of long weekend trips up north to sleep in tents and roast wieners over an open flame. Jacob frowned with embarrassment, remembering how hard he resisted the idea and had sulked all weekend. It had rained and the tent leaked. Once he got wet, he thought he'd never get warm again. He had cried and pouted until Derek packed up the tent and took them to a motel. The next morning, they went home, Derek feeling like a failure and young Jacob, savouring the taste of victory.

Jacob was a man now and he wasn't about to pout or wail, but he could admit that spending long stretches of time in the unpredictable conditions of the great outdoors wasn't for him.

He would keep his word and continue working at the condo building until his two weeks were up. In the meantime, Jacob would give a lot of thought to what he'd like to try next. And he thought maybe it was time to pay a visit to Grandpa's woodworking shop.

CHAPTER THIRTEEN

It was Bob's turn to experience the butterflies of anticipating a new experience.

His meeting at the college with Human Resources manager Jane Witherall was going well, and Bob was enjoying the experience of stepping into the unknown.

Bob didn't need a teaching certificate to be an instructor in construction trades, said Ms. Witherall. Unlike full-time or part-time professors' academic courses, experience was all that counted. Bob's years in the business made him a Ph.D. in construction.

Coming from an academic background, Ms. Witherall knew little — almost nothing, really — about construction or working in the trades, but she was also the facilitator for every other course offered by the college. If a professor left for another job or retired, all eyes turned to her to find a replacement, sometimes based on recommendations from the course coordinator, sometimes not. She was an expert at sourcing experts. It wasn't necessary for her to learn details about what they were experts in.

College was a game of numbers, she told Bob.

"We want our students to learn, of course, and to have long, successful working lives. But frankly, we also *need* them to stay.

Full classrooms are the goal. Any growth in our funding from the province is based on how many registrants we can attract per course and, in turn, how many grads we turn out. It's more complicated than that, but that is the big picture view."

"I get it," said Bob with a nod. "There's no point turning out offering a blacksmithing course if no one's taking it, right?"

"True," said Ms. Witherall, "But it's also about competition. Let's see, there are online courses, and software that promises to teach everything without ever setting foot in a building. Believe it or not, doing nothing is considered competition. However, our biggest competitors are other, similar college courses. If we offer a substandard course, by comparison, our numbers go down, fewer students want to come here and so on."

"Aren't the courses standardized across the board? If you go to College X, don't you get the same education as in College Y, course for course?"

Ms. Witherall shook her head. "There are some standardizations in the macro but not in the micro. Similar courses will more than likely include the same information but there's no mechanism in place to ensure that's the case."

"Wow," Bob replied. "I'm getting an education right now. So, it's partly about keeping these students — and their tuitions — from day one through to getting their certificates?"

"Partly, yes. We always lose a few here and there. Let's face it, some of these kids are only enrolled to keep warm for the winter. Others have unrealistic views of the work that must be done in their chosen field and when they get a reality check, yikes, they're gone. The daydreamers wanted to take a gap year, but their parents told them no. It's our job to deliver engaging, relevant, educational experiences they can take directly into their careers. We have an excellent reputation and an incredibly good placement rate we'd like very much to maintain."

Bob said, "If I read between the lines correctly, you're saying I shouldn't phone it in."

Ms. Witherall smiled. "No one phones it in at Fanshawe. In fact, you'll have a bit of prep work to do. Our last part-time instructor took all his notes and course materials with him. We have no curriculum for the course we'd like you to teach. It's a blank slate. Introduction to Construction is an elective for students in other streams and mandatory for our Construction Project Management students, although some of our more experienced learners can opt-out with 85% on a written exam."

"Okay," said Bob tentatively, "then what are the hours?"

"That's the best part," said Ms. Witherall. "You define them. Your class time is Wednesday afternoons, 1 to 3 pm, but everything else is up to you."

Bob's eyebrows knotted. "So, I can work as many hours as I want? How does that turn out for you? If I did that at my company, I'd go broke."

Ms. Witherall shook her head and looked at Bob patiently. "You're paid for your classroom time. The rest is on your time."

Bob nodded slowly. "Ah, okay, so even the time it takes to make up a curriculum is unpaid. I get it. Marking, too?"

Ms. WItherall nodded.

"Do you have a lot of turnover among part-time faculty, Ms. Witherall?"

Her lips pursed but she didn't respond.

"Okay," Bob mused. "The challenge of designing a course for 15 weeks. . . ."

"Fourteen," interjected Ms. Witherall. "Reading Week falls in your term."

"Fourteen weeks," echoed Bob. It's an interesting task, he thought. And it really wasn't about the money. It was about taking on something he hadn't done before and rising to the occasion. It had been a long time since he had an apprentice to explain things to. He liked the process of showing someone how things were done. And done properly.

"I'll do it," Bob responded firmly.

"Wonderful," said Ms. Witherall. "I'll get the paperwork started and you'll have a couple of weeks to prepare for the class. I will need a course outline then but don't feel you have to have every small detail figured out by that time. We'll put you in our workshop for new faculty. You'll pick up great tips on how to use all the tools we have available at the college and get insight into how students learn. It will be fascinating, I promise, and give you a terrific jump start on your teaching career."

Teaching career, thought Bob, the enormity of what was ahead of him hit him like an electric shock. *What have I done?*

CHAPTER FOURTEEN

Madison thought back to what her father had said whenever she felt overwhelmed by a task. "You eat an elephant one bite at a time." *Time to open wide and take a bite*, she thought.

"Jordan," she began. "Got a minute?"

"Yuh," said Jordan, in that half-listening way people have when their mind and body are occupied with something else.

Jordan was on a ladder, tapping into an electrical line so he could add an outlet to the ceiling. The client had just bought a projector as part of a home theatre system, and he didn't want to see wires hanging from it. Madison had already been up the ladder to see what Jordan was doing. He had crawled into the attic and spliced new wires into a power cable. He threaded those wires through an electrical box and mounted the box between two joists. Now he was on the underside of that part of the job, attaching the other end of the wires to the outlet and preparing to put it in place. Perhaps it wasn't the best time to initiate a conversation, but Jordan was at ease on the ladder. Madison didn't think he'd have a problem twisting wires, testing the current, screwing in the outlet cover, and talking to her at the same time. She'd finally bitten into the elephant, and this was no time to stop chewing.

Madison cleared her throat.

"My grad's coming up soon and I need . . ."

"A chaperone," Jordan interrupted her. "Surely not a date, you know I'm *way* out of your league."

He was looking down at her, his eyes dancing with laughter. Just like a teasing older brother. She knew all about that, having a brother a few years her senior attending university.

"No, geez. I have a serious question to ask you."

"Sorry, Mads, just kidding. What is it? Go ahead."

"Well, like I said, grad is coming up and then I'll be a free agent. And I don't know whether I'm supposed to be invited or if I can just ask. I don't know how it works."

"How what works?" said Jordan, wishing she'd get to the point. "Just spit it out."

"I want to be your apprentice."

Jordan finished screwing in the outlet cover and scurried down the ladder, jumping off the second-to-last step and landing beside her.

"Done," he said, with a grin.

"Oh, that's good. Working overhead is going to take some getting used to but that wasn't so bad."

Jordan laughed heartily. "No, kiddo. Done as in, it will be so. Mr. Turpin already green-lit you. When do you want to start?"

Madison couldn't hide her surprise. Mr. Turpin had already approved of a question she'd just asked 30 seconds ago?

"What do you mean, Mr. Turpin approved?"

"Hey, it's no secret that you like the work and you're a natural. Maybe not with pliers, but you're getting better with practice. So, I asked the boss a hypothetical. If you wanted to apprentice, could I take you on? And he said yes. We've already talked about how there's a huge shortage of skilled tradespeople. He'd bring on five more of you if he could. He will be happy to have you on board."

Madison didn't know what to say. She expected Jordan to have to think about it for a while. Having her underfoot was okay for a month, but was he really prepared to have a Madison-sized shadow for several years? And what about Mr. Turpin? Did he have expectations of her that he hadn't articulated yet? Could she live up to them? Madison's mind swirled with what-ifs. She hadn't told her parents, except in abstract terms. Now she had a way forward and she hadn't consulted them about it. She assumed the pace of acceptance would be slower and that they'd take their time deciding whether to bring her on board. She knew she'd be happy about it once she got over the shock. But would her Mom and Dad?

"Isn't that the answer you wanted?" asked Jordan. "Your forehead is all scrunched up and you're frowning."

Madison relaxed her face and smiled.

"Yes, that's what I wanted, for sure. Thank you. I just didn't expect it to come together so easily. I don't know what I thought. But it's great, yes. Now if you'll just do me a little favour and tell my parents for me," she said with a grin.

"Oh no," Jordon said, holding out his palms toward her. "No way, Jose. I've been through that and once is enough, thank you."

Madison tilted her head. "Wait a minute. Are you telling me you had a hard time telling your parents that you wanted to be an electrician? Really?"

"You mean, Dr. Abigail Lattan, dermatologist and Dr. Gabriel Lattan, orthopedic surgeon? Oh, no, not at all," said Jordan, with mock seriousness.

"Oh, I had no idea," Madison said.

"And then there's my older brother, Dr. Michael Lattan, ophthalmologist. And my uncle, Dr. Grant Lattan, research scientist. Do you want me to continue?"

"So, your future was planned out and you didn't go along with the plan."

Jordan nodded. "That's one way of putting it. Another way is my Mother's take, that I drove a stake through her heart and crushed her dreams for a successful future for me."

"They laid it on thick, huh."

"Like mayo on a ham sandwich. It's all good now but it took a few years for them to come around. They could only see one path for themselves and for their kids. If you were smart, you became a doctor, end of story. I think way down deep my Mom still hopes I'll go to med school. But on the surface, she's fine with it now."

"She must see that you've done all right."

"Giving her a couple of grandkids didn't hurt. But over the years she's talked to other people who have a lot of respect for the trades. My parents' friends built a house and they raved about the contractor and everyone on the build, how professional and polite they were. My Mom made it sound like a huge revelation. That's progress, I guess."

"Got any tips for me when I tell my parents?"

Jordon thought for a moment. "Tell them how it compares to other jobs where people get downsized and shown the door for no reason at all. There's more work than we can handle and it's not going to ebb and flow to keep a bunch of shareholders happy. Mads, there are no guarantees in life. But you're good at this, you're a fast learner, and as far as anyone can see, there will always be a market for your skills. And your parents won't have to put their lives on hold so you can go to university for four years.

Or if you're paying for it yourself, you can avoid working around the clock or accumulating debt and living on credit — all of that stuff that can keep people from getting a good foothold in life."

"They should be able to see that it makes sense."

"Yeah, they should," said Jordan, "and if they don't, well, it might be a little uncomfortable for a while. But it's more uncomfortable to hate getting up for work every day. I helped around my Dad's office sometimes, and I thought I'd climb out the window just to get some air and get away from the stuffy atmosphere. I hated it. That was enough proof for me."

"I think they always pictured themselves at my graduation with a rolled-up diploma in my hand, and me throwing my cap in the air, like a movie or something."

"Make a new movie for them. They don't have to give up on their dreams for you, but you have your own dreams. Maybe you can all meet in the middle."

Madison sighed heavily. "I hope so. Thanks for the advice. So, it does get better, right?"

"Yup. Just get on with things and don't worry too much about it. I did some work at my parents' house and now they call me doctor too. Dr. Juice. At first, I think it was a gentle way of mocking me for not becoming a doctor, but now it's my thing. If anyone in the family has a question about electricity or anything to do with their house, they call Dr. Juice. Silly."

Madison shrugged. "Whatever works. Wish me luck."

"Good luck," said Jordan. "It'll be fine."

"Whatever you say, doctor."

CHAPTER FIFTEEN

Jacob ambled down the high school corridor, carefully dodging out of the way of fellow students who were moving at a faster pace. Jacob felt more at ease at school these days. It was like the day-to-day stresses of high school life had less meaning now that he was putting more focus on his future. What did it matter if history teacher Mr. Portelli surprised the students with a pop quiz? It would all be over soon enough, and he'd be starting a new career. He was an adult, and adults didn't worry about the stuff of kids. He was looking at his hand, palm up, and admiring the callouses he'd gotten, when he heard his name.

It was Fuaads from algebra class, a fellow student he knew by name but that's where it ended. Jacob sat in the back row during algebra, low in his seat, trying to go unnoticed. Fuaads sat in the front row, alert, with perfect posture. He was a math whiz, while Jacob's arithmetic skills didn't extend far beyond using a measuring tape and changing the adage, "measure twice cut once" to "measure a half dozen times, prepare to cut, then measure again." He did okay in algebra, though, and compared to his fellow students who saw no purpose in it, he knew that it would become useful for working out angles and other aspects of carpentry.

"Hi," said Fuaads. "Do you have one minute?"

"I guess," said Jacob.

Fuaads motioned Jacob to step out of the stream of teenage traffic and closer to the lockers so they could talk.

"I am hearing that you are involved with a carpentry program."

"Well," said Jacob, "it's more of a job-shadowing program. I picked carpentry but there are all sorts of other things to try, like HVAC, electrical, plumbing — tons of stuff."

"I see," said Fuaads. "My parents, since I was a little boy, they have told me that I am to become the first college graduate in our family. I am having doubts."

"Doubts about what. About what you want to study? Or college?"

"Doubts about all of it, my friend. Attending school for many more years, full-time. My father was laid off from his accounting firm and has not yet found another job. My mother works part-time and it's not enough income for the rent and the food and the utilities. They made this promise to me when I was a small child and now it is not affordable. I want to ease their burden and help my family. I want to do what you are doing. Job shading."

"Shadowing," said Jacob. "It's called Ride and Decide. You could do it if you wanted to."

"Do you think so?"

"For sure. Make an appointment with the Guidance Counsellor. Ask him about it. He'll get you set up."

Fuaads' face brightened. "Okay, I will do that. Thank you, Jacob. Thank you very much."

Jacob waved his hand as if to say, "it's nothing." He continued down the corridor, whistling happily.

CHAPTER SIXTEEN

Jordan did it and his family's full of doctors. I can do this. I can do this.

Madison gave herself a silent pep talk before opening the subject of her future with her parents. She was in the hallway outside her family's living room where her mom and dad were both quietly reading. Her Mom was curled up in a huge, round chair flipping through Madison's copy of *Mother Earth News*. Her Dad, on his back on the leather couch, holding a tablet above his head, was reading business news.

Before she lost her nerve, Madison forced herself to make a sharp right and face her parents for what she predicted would be a difficult conversation. She plopped into an armchair beside the fireplace and waited to be noticed.

"Hi sweetie," said her father absentmindedly without taking his eyes off the tablet.

"Hey, Mads," said her Mom, laying the magazine on her lap. "Anything new?"

"How do you like the magazine?" Madison asked her mom.

Her Mom nodded and said, "it's interesting. I think I could make an herb garden out of some pallet wood now. And a composting toilet, although I might need to read those instructions a couple more times."

"Yuck," said her dad, his eyes still locked on an article about cryptocurrency.

Madison swallowed hard.

"Can we talk a minute?"

Her father lowered the tablet and made brief eye contact with his wife before looking at his daughter.

"Sure honey," he said. "Sounds serious."

"It kinda is," said Madison.

"Everything okay?" asked her mother.

"Oh yeah, nothing to worry about. Nothing's wrong. I just want to talk to you about something. It's important to me."

Her father sat up and placed the tablet on the coffee table. "If it's important to you, it's important to us. So, what's the issue? Or the problem? Or the topic, I guess?"

"Well, you know I'll be graduating high school soon. . . ."

"I know what this is about," said Madison's mother, cutting off her daughter in mid-sentence. "Our little girl here wants to work with the boys and become an electrician. She wants to wear combat boots and a hard hat and get her lunch from a truck window, isn't that right, Madison?"

"Well, it's not like that really, Mom, it's. . . ."

Her father interjected. "What's this? An electrician? Gail, do you know how much electricians cost? And have you ever tried to find one? We'd have an electrician in the family — how cool is that!"

"Robert!" admonished her mother.

"Oh, now calm down, Gail. For goodness' sake. It's a wonderful choice. Are you sure this is what you want, honey? I know you're enjoying the job shadow, but the job is another thing altogether."

"That's the thing, Dad, it really isn't. I'm out on real calls, getting experience working for real clients! This *is* the job. And I love it."

"You *love* it," said Madison's Mom, her voice thick with sarcasm. "What else have you even tried to do? You haven't given anything else a chance. Far be it from me to want my daughter to wear a dress and carry a purse to her job, instead of jeans and a lunch pail!"

"I thought it was combat boots and a lunch truck," said her dad.

"Oh, Robert." She burst into tears.

"Mom, I told you it's more than that. I also told you that I feel like I belong. I love it. And I'm not looking into anything else because I don't want to *do* anything else. I don't want to push papers around or look at a computer all day. That's not me. I feel like this job makes a difference. I don't have to become a different person to do it."

"How does putting on nice clothes make you a different person?" asked her mom.

"I like nice clothes but that's not what a career is about. Who cares what I wear anyway? And Mom, they're steel-toed safety boots. Not combat boots. What I wear should be about being comfortable and protected. That's what clothing is for."

"She's right, Gail. Otherwise, I'd be in a loincloth and not much else. They'd frown on that at the office. Definitely not the dress code."

"How can you joke at a time like this," asked Gail, drying her eyes by pressing them with the backs of her hands.

"Because it's not the end of the world. And if for whatever reason she decided it wasn't what she wanted, after all, that wouldn't be the end of the world either. She's young. She should try things out now before a mortgage and family come into the picture."

Gail pursed her lips.

"Mom," Madison pleaded, "I asked Jordan if I could be his apprentice and it's been approved. I can start right away. I'll have to enroll in trade school, but it will cost almost nothing. I'll get paid during the working months and collect EI while I'm in school. I was thinking, maybe, my college fund could go into a down payment for a rental house instead. I could live there, have a couple of roommates, and fix it up. The rent I collect would carry it and it would create equity pretty quick."

Her Dad said, "Mads, it's an education fund. We only started calling it a college fund because that's what we figured you'd do. Go to college. Or university. But it's for whatever you want, so the school of life it is."

He looked at his wife. She attempted a weak smile, but her eyes betrayed her. She was deeply disappointed and trying not to show it.

"Oh, Mads. I know your dad is right. You should do what you want. Become whomever you want to be." She paused and Madison knew her Mom wanted to say more, so she waited silently.

"You don't know what it's like to be a parent and have so many hopes and dreams for your child. I really do want you to be happy. I just can't get excited about this. Yet. But I'll work on it. I'm sure your dad will work on it, too."

The couple exchanged warm smiles.

"Thank you! Thank you, thank you. I'm going to make you so proud!"

Madison leapt out of her chair and onto her mother's. She grabbed her mother around the neck and gave her a squeeze. Then she backed off the chair and did the same to her dad.

"You'll be great, kiddo," he said. "We love our little girl."

Madison bounded out of the living room and ran toward her bedroom where she flopped on the bed, grabbing her phone from the dresser as she went. She opened text messages and began typing to Jordan:

Hello Dr. Juice. It looks like you'll have some help in the ER! They said YES!

CHAPTER SEVENTEEN

From electrician to managing contractor to part-time college instructor. Bob couldn't have imagined the places his career would take him and didn't even try to guess what might come next. He and his wife had talked about going overseas once the kids were out on their own and loaning their skills to home-building programs for underserved areas of the world. Bob had already done some informal consulting on projects for other companies. He could pursue that as a later-life business venture if he so desired. He enjoyed advising less-experienced colleagues partly because it reminded him of how much knowledge he'd amassed over the years. Nothing was quite as satisfying as the moment when something Bob said cleared up confusion for someone else. When the person said, "*Oh,*" and their whole demeanour altered from frustrated to clear understanding, it gave Bob a kick. It was a great experience.

That's what Bob hoped to get more of with this new teaching gig. But first, he had to decide what to teach. He knew from the college's weekend-long program for new instructors that it was up to him to meet the student's expectations about learning. Some were more visual, others auditory, and still others preferred to absorb knowledge from a good old-fashioned book. It was a great departure from the days when Bob was in school. Back then, the onus was on the student to learn, not on the instructor to teach them in the specific and individual way they needed to be taught. He would have to come up with a mix of PowerPoint presentations, some YouTube videos, some reading and, he decided, some opportunities to get the students' hands dirty.

Introduction to Construction was a vague title that could cover a huge range of things found on a wide variety of construction sites. Bob closed his eyes and thought back to when he started working on new home builds. What did he not know? What did he need to know? And what would have been great to know that no one bothered to tell him until he learned it the hard way?

On a large notepad, he wrote a list of the numbers 1 to 14, standing for the classes. Safety first, he thought, as he scribbled the words next to number 1. Going over the gear and the reasons for wearing it. To keep it from becoming boring he'd list all the ways a person could get hurt on a construction site, including the materials in use and the types of work being done. That would double as an overview of what the students could expect to learn in his course. Next to number 13, he wrote "field trip" before scratching it out and rewriting the words next to number 12. They'd need class 13 as a refresher before the final exam in the final class. He made a mental note to decide which of his building sites would still have lots of different work underway for the field trip and which one was best for a crowd of two dozen eager students to visit.

He knew that one hurdle in the way of explaining the reality of construction was popular TV shows that gave the perception that a home could get properly built in a few days. Rarely did they show inspectors or delays in material deliveries. Whether it was a renovation, or a structure being built from the ground up, in the real world you never saw a collection of supermodels wielding sledgehammers and reciprocating saws wearing midriff-baring tops and tight jeans. So much of what happens gets edited out of those shows. Bob scribbled a note to remind himself to touch on that topic.

Ideas swirled around in his mind. He tried to grab onto them and arrange them in some sort of order. Slowly, the course outline revealed itself to him, and he knew what he had to do to prepare beyond breaking it down class by class. He needed to go shopping.

CHAPTER EIGHTEEN

The single garage door was wide open when Jacob arrived to visit his grandfather, whom he called Grandpa Jake. The tall, distinguished-looking man, with grey hair and a trimmed, grey beard, was decked out in a leather apron that looked like it had never previously been worn. He gave the appearance of a model in a retirement residence ad. His grandad waved, as Jacob parked next to the curb and got out of his car carrying a white box.

"What have you got there?" asked Jacob's grandfather, as Jacob got closer.

"A box of donuts," Jacob said, sheepishly. "Mom said you like 'em, and Grandma doesn't let you have 'em, so it would be a treat." He held out the box toward his grandfather.

"It is indeed." Jake took the donuts and set them on a workbench. "I'll enjoy these. Thanks, lad."

"Welcome," said Jacob. He took in the scene, noting all the machines were set up and ready to go with demonstration pieces of wood strategically placed around the garage. His grandpa must have been up since 5 am to prepare for this. It never occurred to Jacob that the old man might be looking forward to their morning together, too.

Jacob's grandad clapped his hands and rubbed them together in anticipation.

"Okay, then. Shall we begin? I thought we'd go through the major tools and some of the most common cuts and joints you'll need to make. We'll start at the bench."

Jacob followed his grandfather who was moving at a brisk pace, despite only having to take six strides to reach the workbench. It was about eight feet long and counter-height with a white laminate top that was chipped around the edges. Jacob expected a layer of dust and wood shavings. He noticed brushes and dustpans hanging from nails at each end of the table, and a large, garbage-bag-lined container full of shavings and wood scraps. Grandpa Jake liked things tidy.

Grandpa Jake held up a large plastic bottle with a thick, pale yellow liquid inside.

"This is wood glue. Wood glue is your friend. You'll want to squeeze this stuff onto joints like you got it for free. Let it run down the sides of your project. Doesn't matter. You can always wipe it up. But if you don't use enough, you can get into trouble."

"Be generous with the wood glue. Got it," said Jacob.

Jake pointed to a tall plastic cabinet with plenty of see-through drawers and tiny, hand-written labels.

"There are your nails, screws, washers, all your hardware, sorted by size and type. Don't be fooled by what they're called. See this?"

He held up a small, dark screw.

"This is a drywall screw. But you can use it for other things besides drywall. Same with deck screws, et cetera. Use the right screw for the right job. You'll figure that out as you go along."

Jacob nodded, wondering how many types of screws there were in the world, but not wanting to potentially embarrass himself by asking. That's what Google was for.

"And then," said Grandpa Jake, "there are your screwdrivers, your drills with driver bits, all of those are more-or-less common in most households. Save your wrist. Use the battery-powered tools when you can. Does Derek have a lot of tools?"

Jacob shook his head. His stepfather wasn't a fan of DIY projects around the home or fixing things for that matter. He'd rather get dropped in the woods with a knife and need to whittle his own hammer.

"Naw," Jacob said. "He's not a big tool guy."

"Okay. Well, you're welcome to come over here and use these any time, if I'm around to supervise. Some of them almost look like toys but I assure you, they are not. You can get hurt if you don't know what you're doing. In fact, I'm going to need you to put on these glasses before we power anything up, please."

Jake handed his grandson a pair of oversized, clear, plastic glasses and Jacob put them on. They felt comically large, but the sides met his temples, and he knew they'd keep flying debris out of his eyes.

Over the course of the next couple of hours, Jacob's grandfather showed him how to run a table saw, a band saw, a router, a lathe, and a mitre saw. Lastly, Grandpa Jake held firm to a piece of wood while he instructed Jacob to cut it with a hand saw. The teeth of the blade kept getting stuck in the wood. It was hard labour compared to using a power saw, but Jacob kept at it until he cut through.

"Notice the finished job, here," said Grandpa Jake, pointing to the freshly cut ends. "You'd get better with practice, for sure, but it's not cut as cleanly as the machine could do it."

With panting breaths, Jacob said, "What was the point of that?"

Jake laughed. "To show you that you've got it good! And to give you a taste of how difficult carpentry used to be. That was only pine, lad. Imagine cutting through hardwood. Now, when you look closely at a cabinet that was built 150 years ago and notice how tight the corners are and how well it's made, you'll be able to appreciate the artistry and sweat that went into it. That's why antiques last so long and your prefab, manufactured fake-wood furniture falls apart easily."

"Wow, yeah. For sure," said Jacob. "I never thought of that."

"That's what us old guys are for, lad."

"Thanks, Grandpa. Today has been great. This is what I want to do. Cabinetmaking."

"Well, get to it then. And maybe you'll come over here and show me a trick or two someday. Here, have a donut. You earned it."

Jacob grabbed a cruller from the box and chomped into it greedily. His grandfather chose a plain old-fashioned.

Jacob swallowed. "Hey Grandpa Jake, can I ask you a question?"

"Certainly."

"Doesn't Grandma want to park her car in the garage? I mean, in the rain and snow and stuff?"

Grandpa Jake replied with a smile. "Oh, she wants to, she definitely wants to. But this is part of the deal we made when we got married. Garages aren't for cars. They're for workshops. We're 46 years into this marriage, and I think she's finally given up on ever parking her car under a cover. If the snow gets really bad in the winter, I'll go out and brush off her car for her. It's all a trade-off."

CHAPTER NINETEEN

It was Kevin's favourite type of morning for a run. The air was crisp and cool. Most people would grab a jacket before heading out on such a day, but Kevin was feeling comfortable in his T-shirt and baggy shorts. Once he worked up a sweat, he was almost too warm. The day promised sunshine and heat. He loved getting out before going to work and thinking about everything or nothing as he ran.

On this run, he was ruminating over a recent meeting with Bob Turpin, his boss. He'd laid it all out factually for Bob. HVAC was getting busier — demand was growing for all aspects of Bob's business — and Kevin thought it was best for all concerned if he and Tim divided and conquered. Kevin liked working with Tim. They'd developed a communication style where they almost finished each others' sentences. But thinking about his career, Kevin decided the next logical step was for him to partner with a junior service tech, maybe even take on an apprentice. He articulated this to Bob whose disappointment was obvious.

"Do you think it's a bad idea?" asked Kevin.

Bob had raised his palms. "No, Kev, not at all. It's a great idea. I want to grow this division, too, and you're right. You're more than ready for this. The problem is finding people. We're lucky we have Madison apprenticing in electrical. We lost Jacob to carpentry. We have to cast wider nets and find the right folks, but the truth is, we're too darn busy to go from school to school. We can't do it all alone. And you know it's not easy dispelling preconceived notions about the trades. It's getting better but it's not over. Not by a long shot."

Kevin had looked at the floor. He knew what Bob was saying was true, but it didn't make it any easier to hear.

"I have goals of my own, too," Kevin had said. "And I can't meet them unless there are people coming up behind me who need training and experience. It's frustrating."

"I get it," Bob had replied. "And I really wish I could do something to change it. You know Wilson Rentals? They rent and fix everything and anything with a motor. Shutting down. 45 years in business and they're closing up because they can't find small engine mechanics to replace the guys who are retiring. They are a busy shop, and they can't keep going with only current staff. The auction's next week."

Kevin had shaken his head sadly. "I don't know what this means for me. I like the job, I do, but I have to be able to see another rung on the ladder. Something to reach for, you know. It's just how I'm wired."

"Again, I get it. I'm seeing kids who are already getting priced out of owning a home, not even able to save up for a down payment because of their student loans. All because they thought college or university was their only route to success. It will be years before they're on a level playing field with our new guys. We just need more of them. I'm open to ideas for recruitment. We have those videos on YouTube, and the testimonials you did a few years ago. But that's not enough when someone like you comes to me and says they want to move up. If I could make it happen, I would. All I can tell you is, when it's possible, we'll do it."

"Best I can hope for right now, I suppose," Kevin had said.

As he rounded the corner onto his street, Kevin reminded himself to be grateful that his boss had his back. But he didn't know how long he could wait for things to get better.

CHAPTER TWENTY

Now that she was officially part of a working team, Madison felt less intimidated on the job site. Jordan had always been great about introducing her to colleagues and making her feel at ease, but she realized she'd been hiding in his shadow. She was an apprentice with a title and a purpose. She no longer felt like a kid following an adult around, like a duckling and duck.

She had been reading about common electrical problems and hoped to see knob and tube wiring for herself in the near future. It crossed her mind that most of the old houses may have been upgraded and her chances of experiencing a retrofit were dimming. She hoped she was wrong.

Madison was surprised to read how dangerous it was to rely on cheap, thin extension cords and power strips long term. Her Dad put dollar store power strips all over the house when what it really needed were more places to plug into the walls. She decided to install a bunch of new outlets for her parents as soon as she was certified to do so. Maybe she'd make it a Christmas present. In the meantime, she'd talk to her dad about unplugging a few things when he wasn't using them. It was a start.

She had always had questions for Jordan and now she had a million new ones about trade school. She'd be signing up soon. He had already told her that she should expect to be in class for three terms, total — 2 lasting 10 weeks each and one lasting 8 weeks. The rest of the time she'd get hands-on experience with Jordan until her 9000 hours were up. It would take a little more than 4 years.

Her formal schooling would cost little, especially compared to a college certificate or university degree. The government offered interest-free loans and grants that she'd investigate right away. Her pay wasn't a lot, but it was still an income, and she almost couldn't believe her good fortune. Madison felt as if she'd stumbled on a secret to getting launched into adulthood by catapult compared to most of her peers who were slowly ambling their way along. She searched hard for a downside and couldn't come up with one as she buckled her tool belt and pulled her hard hat on. With her mom and dad now on board, more or less, she felt unstoppable.[4]

---

4 Ontario government financial support for apprentices. https://www.ontario.ca/page/financial-supports-apprentices#:~:text=Apprenticeship%20Incentive%20Grant,for%20at%20least%2012%20months

CHAPTER TWENTY-ONE

The day of Bob's first class at the college finally arrived and he felt prepared and excited. The course had been a blank slate and Bob found the prospect of filling it a little daunting after so many decades of following plans and instructions. He had sat looking at a blank computer screen for a long while before deciding to write down everything he thought of, with no judgement, just to get the creative juices flowing. He laughed now thinking about his craziest idea — a rap based on the rhyming properties of the title — Introduction to Construction. That concept didn't get far before he tossed it out. But that's what brainstorming was for, to ramp up the ideas and keep only the good ones.

The teaching methods course for instructors administered by the college had been valuable. Essentially, it advised him to mix it up. Do some lecturing, some power-points, film, and tactile experiences. Individuals learn in different ways, and it was up to instructors to meet the students' expectations, not the other way around. Quite a different approach from when the days when Bob was in school when teachers were kings and queens, and it was up to the serfs to figure everything out.

He had finished the course outline, and the first three sessions had been approved by the college. That's how it worked, according to administrators who were overloaded with work, and in some cases, heavy course loads of their own. They'd get a chance to review the rest of the outline as the semester went on.

Students would get a surprise if they expected a lot of dull reading. Over the coming weeks, Bob planned to get their hands dirty. He had a small budget for materials that he stretched by bringing in some leftover and damaged items from work. He arrived at the college early with a loaded pickup and a hand cart and began piling things and hauling them into the classroom.

When students arrived, they would notice a collection of stuff in one corner of the room, including a bag of cement mix, a pile of bricks, pieces of drywall, spatulas, various adhesives, and stacks of protective goggles and gloves. This "introduction" course was going to be more than a handshake and a how-do-you-do.

Bob was excited, a little nervous, and hoping to inspire his students. He'd keep to himself the fanciful daydreams of being the Robin Williams character in *Dead Poets Society*. He didn't really expect students to cheer his arrival. But maybe a few of them would become interested enough in the topic to carry through with a career in one of the trades. He also hoped to discover one or two who had natural talent.

Bob was always on the lookout for people to add to his staff or his list of trusted sub-contractors, or to recommend to colleagues in the industry. Students from an introductory course weren't likely to be prime prospects but he'd keep his ears open, just in case. Sometimes life experience was almost as valuable as education. Having pored over the student list beforehand, he knew it included a few mature adults returning to the classroom to retrain for a new career. Four of the 28 students were women. Most had come straight from high school. Maybe there'd be a go-getter among the bunch?

The computer was ready to go with his power-point presentation. He checked his watch again, feeling like the new kid at a strange school, which he supposed was right. He sat at the desk and opened his briefcase. Inside, along with business cards, papers, and other odds and ends, was a big, red apple his wife had left beside the coffeemaker, with a post-It note that read, "For my favourite teacher." Bob shined the apple on his pants leg, opened wide and took a bite.

CHAPTER TWENTY-TWO

Shaker, beaded, farmhouse, craftsman, traditional, contemporary, and more. Jacob studied pages of images of cabinet door styles online. And then there were materials: maple, cherry, mahogany, fibreboard, ash, pine, and oak, to name a few. Stained, unstained, painted, natural, lacquered, dark, light, medium – so many options available to clients, they made his head spin. And he hadn't even considered dimensions yet. Or glass inserts. And any number of other things he wasn't aware of yet.

Jacob's thoughts were interrupted by his phone buzzing on his desk beside him. He hit answer and then speaker.

"Hullo?"

"I'm looking for Jacob," said a male voice.

"I'm Jacob."

"Great. Jacob, I'm a friend of your grandfather's. Actually, the son of a friend of your grandfather. Louis Harland. We're in the same woodworking group."

"Woodworking group? I didn't know my grandpa was in one."

"Oh yeah, The Wood Nuts. We get together and noodle around, make stuff for charity bazaars, bowls, kid's toys, things like that.

Everyone pitches in scrap wood, and we try to do something useful with it. It's just for fun, not profit."

"Cool," said Jacob. "He never mentioned it."

"Well, it's a little like bragging, now, isn't it? In my case, it's an opportunity to keep the creative juices flowing. Step outside the box, no pun intended."

Jacob snickered.

"Anyway," the voice continued, "your grandad told me about showing you around his shop and that you're fairly sure you want to be a cabinet maker. Is that the case?"

"Yes," Jacob replied. "I'm completely sure. I love working with wood and making stuff with my hands. It's . . . interesting," he said, wishing he could find a better way to express himself.

"It's all that and a box of crackers!" Louis Harland laughed heartily.

"So, what can I do for you, Mr. Harland? I don't quite know why you're calling me."

"Oh, yes. I suppose I should end the mystery! I own a company called Kitchens Kitchens Kitchens. It's not difficult to figure out what we do! And I need a cabinetmaker. You'd need to apprentice. I wanted to offer you a position at my shop and pair you up with one of my journeymen. We've brought on several apprentices over the years, and we can guide you through the process. There's plenty of work. A big variety of projects. Little renos and big builds. Jake says you're a strong young man and can haul some stuff around. The rest of it comes with practice."

Jacob was struck dumb. This was it. The door to his future was just kicked wide open.

"Are you there, son? Do you . . . have any questions?"

"N—n—no, sir," Jacob finally stammered. "Not right now, I don't. My mind is a total blank. Sure, I'd love to be an apprentice at Kitchens Kitchens Kitchens. Thank you so much for the opportunity."

"Great!" said Louis. "And you can just call it Kitchens. Saves time that way."

"Okay," said Jacob. "When do I start?"

"That depends. When do you want to start?"

"Now?" said Jacob, only half-kidding.

"Haha! No, you cool your jets for a bit and come see us Monday. You've got the CSA-approved safety gear, right?"

"Everything but a hard hat."

"I'll get you one of those. Okay, we'll see you dark and early Monday morning. 7 am. I hope that won't be a problem."

"No sir," said Jacob, confident he'd be awake at 6 am, excited to get the day underway.

"See you then, Jacob. Looking forward to having you on the team."

Jacob said thank you again and ended the call. He was still in shock that he was about to become a real apprentice and begin his journey toward becoming a cabinetmaker. He remembered a talk his high school guidance counsellor had given to his class about job hunting.

"75 percent of the job market is hidden," the man had said. "It's a matter of who you know, your connections, getting the word out, and letting people know that you're looking for work."

Lucky for Jacob, the only person he had needed to tell was his grandfather, and he wasn't even aware that he had been networking. Jacob picked up his phone and punched in his grandparents' phone number. He needed to deliver another "thank you" and then get back to researching the elements of his new career.

CHAPTER TWENTY-THREE

When Bob Turpin founded Turpin General Contractors, he vowed to do things differently. Having worked for several different contractors in his earlier career as an electrician, Bob knew what employees hated and what they loved. They hated feeling overbooked and pressured to do a two-hour job in 90 minutes. They loved free stuff.

One of the Turpin traditions was beloved by everyone on staff. Once a site was dug out, leveled, and ready for construction to begin, everyone who would eventually be part of the team was expected to meet there. They'd get a couple days' notice about a Site Meeting and turn up first thing in the morning. Sometimes it created extra work to reschedule a residential job that had been booked for that morning, but it was worth it.

Once employees started arriving, they'd be treated to breakfast. Bob would hire two or three food trucks to come out and cook hot meals of waffles, bacon, pancakes, and eggs served with great coffee. There'd be laughter and gossip as workers who rarely saw each other had a chance to catch up. The "work" part of this off-site meeting was Bob's quick overview of the project. Otherwise, it was a social event disguised as a mandatory assignment. Bob loved seeing how much everyone enjoyed themselves. It was a break from the routine that people looked forward to.

Bob's accountant once questioned him about the expenditure. The first few such meetings had been held at company HQ with a chef in the tiny lunchroom kitchen serving breakfast.

"You know, you could pick up a few boxes of muffins and donuts and you'd still be a hero," the accountant had said.

"What fun is that?" asked Bob. "That's not special enough. I want it to feel like some effort was made, at least."

The accountant shrugged. "Donuts can be heavy."

"Hilarious," mumbled Bob in a tone that meant it wasn't hilarious at all.

"Okay, do me one favour? No, make it two. Keep your receipts, and talk about work at some point, in some capacity? Otherwise, it's not a work event, but a work party. I don't want your tax returns raising any eyebrows because you're throwing more expensive than average monthly work parties."

That's when the idea of moving festivities off site to a build-in-progress came to Bob. He added a short address to his staff about the project, and that made his accountant happy. It was true that he didn't have to spend so much at these Site Meetings, but he could afford to do it because of his employees, and he wanted to show his appreciation to everyone for their hard work.

Occasionally, in this less formal setting, an employee would take Bob aside and complain about something or another. A frustrating aspect of the job or a minor beef with a colleague. But Bob thought that was valuable too. Better they bring a problem to his attention so he could correct it, rather than leave the company in a silent huff. Sometimes they wanted his ear so they could share a way they'd found to save money or time. Bob gave them his attention and consideration, even if what they were proposing was next to impossible. Sometimes, they just wanted to be heard. People were Turpin General Contractors' greatest resource — valuable, and difficult to find new ones when he needed them.

CHAPTER TWENTY-FOUR

Madison was curled up on the living-room sofa, half-watching TV with her parents. Her mom had insisted on streaming *Gilmore Girls* again. What was this, the third time? The show was amusing enough, Madison supposed, but she didn't get the attraction of repeated viewings. She guessed that her mom liked the familiarity of it, like pulling an old sweater around her shoulders. "There's always something new that I missed the last time around," her mom had said.

In this episode, Luke, who ran the town of Stars Hollow's popular diner, was being asked to come back to his high school to talk about being successful in business. Luke was famously grumpy about town events and socializing in general. Madison's ears perked up at one of the character's comments as he reminisced about not being a great student.

"I'm sure my high school transcripts file is stamped 'trade school.' "

Ouch thought Madison. *That's an outdated, not to mention incorrect cliché about going to trade school.* She couldn't help but feel personally offended and wondered if her mom caught the insinuation. If she did, to Madison's relief she wasn't showing it.

Where did the idea of trade school being a last-resort possibility for kids with poor grades even come from, Madison wondered. She opened the Google app on her phone and punched in, trade school beliefs. Several versions of a 2019 high school survey showed up.[5] She clicked on one and discovered that negative thoughts about trade schools were mostly born out of ignorance. In a national survey of American adults aged 18-24, more than half said they didn't learn about trade schools in high school. Two-thirds said their guidance counsellor never discussed it. Half said they'd rather be a barista (earning minimum wage) than a welder (potentially earning $100,000 or more) just because of negative perceptions of people who work with their hands. *As if baristas make coffee with their feet*, Madison thought.

Madison chewed on the survey results as Lorelai and Rory Gilmore traded rapid fire sentences about something banal, likely coffee because it was their favourite subject. The survey respondents' answers weren't fair, and they didn't even make sense. There was nothing wrong with being a barista, but it didn't even compare to plumbing or electrical or welding when it came to knowledge and skill. Why could she see this so clearly, but others her age could not? *Gilmore Girls* was an older show, so she forgave its writers for Luke's remark. The survey, however, was just two years old.

Change had to begin somewhere, and Madison decided it should start with her writing an email to her old high school Principal, Mr. Mings. If she could convince him to put trade schools in the guidance counsellor's list of options for grads to consider,

---

5 Survey: Lack of Awareness and Negative Perceptions of Trade Schools and Careers. https://www.metalsupermarkets.com/survey-says-there-is-a-lack-of-awareness-and-negative-perception-of-trade-schools-and-careers/

it would be a good start. The *Gilmore Girls* were still talking at top speed as Madison opened her email app and began writing her passionate plea to Mr. Mings.

CHAPTER TWENTY-FIVE

The school's guidance counsellor was happy to make a couple of phone calls on Fuaads' behalf, to get him into a Ride and Decide program. Fuaads thought it was odd that he'd never heard about Ride and Decide until Jacob told him about it. It seemed like an opportunity that all students should be made aware of, especially at a time when they were being pressed from all sides to decide about their future. If not for Jacob, Fuaads might not have ever thought about doing something other than following the path that was laid out for him. He would enrol in Ride and Decide, but his mind was already made up — he was going to become a plumber.

All that was left was the matter of talking to his parents about his decision. His future was rarely discussed at home because it had been decided when he was young. He would go to university, earn a degree, get a great job, get married, have a family, and live a happy life, in that order. No one talked about it because it was understood by all parties. What was there to discuss?

Now that Fuaads' father had been out of work for a long time, Fuaads knew there was a strain on his parents as he got closer to graduation. His parents had promised to fund his university education, and now it seemed that would be impossible. Fuaads couldn't bear to think of his parents stressing out over his future. But he braced himself for a bad reaction. His announcement would change everything about their lives and quite possibly put a dent in his father's fierce pride.

"Mother, Father, I need to speak with you, please," Fuaads said after he got home from school. His mother was at the stove stirring a large pot of khichdi while his father sat at the kitchen table reading a newspaper.

"What is it, Fuaads? Are you all right? Are you sick?"

"No mother, I am fine. I need to talk to you about something important."

His mother tapped the spoon on the rim of the pot and set it on the counter. She wiped her hands on her apron and joined her husband at the table. Fuaads' father lowered his newspaper and peered over it at his son.

"What is the matter, boy?" he said. "Out with it."

Fuaads pulled out a chair and sat across from his parents. He was nervous and his mouth felt like sandpaper. He briefly thought about saying, "Never mind," and going up to his room, but he knew that putting this off would only make things worse in the long run. He folded his hands on the table in front of him.

"Soon, I will graduate—"

"Yes, with honours!" his father interjected.

"That's true, father. With honours. And I've been thinking about my future."

"You will go to university," said his mother, proudly.

"That's what I want to talk about. I don't *have* to go to university."

The newspaper rattled as his father slammed his knuckles on the table. "What do you mean you don't have to go? Of course, you have to go! You must go!"

Fuaads willed himself to stay calm in the face of his father's outburst. He did not want this conversation to devolve into a shouting match like discussions with his dad sometimes had in the past. That would do nothing.

"I know that you both want me to attend university. But what if there was another way for me to get an education and start a career? A good paying career, Father. And one that I am interested in?"

"I'm listening," said his father, visibly calming.

"I learned about this program where I can try out a new career. See how I like it. Find out whether I'm good at it. And it's something I want to do."

His mother asked, "How can you "try out" a career? What kind of career? This doesn't sound like a good career."

"It is, Mother, it is. It's something every person will need at some point in their lives."

"A doctor? You can try out becoming a doctor? This is nonsense."

"No, not a doctor. A plumber. I want to become a plumber."

Fuaads' father said, "A plumber? Why? Why a plumber, Fuaads?"

Fuaads shrugged. "I don't know. I like the idea of fixing something and making it better than it was. It's helping people, like a doctor, but no one dies."

His mother nodded solemnly. "No one dies in plumbing. That is true."

Fuaads continued. “It’s less schooling. And I would get paid while I learned on the job with someone who is experienced at plumbing. It’s a different type of school. And there are grants that I can apply for. It would be almost free. I really want to do it.”

Fuaads’ father shook his head slowly. “That sounds too good to be true, Fuaads.”

“I know. But there are lots of jobs and not enough people to do them. The government is trying to get students like me to follow this type of path, and I can see why. There will always be work in this field. And right now, those who are working cannot keep up with the demand.”

“Let me understand. You can start working right away, get paid to work while you learn, and take classes for free? Is that what you’re saying?”

“Yes, father. I know how it sounds, but it’s true. I can show you all of the documentation. And it’s work that I want to do.”

Fuaads’ mother rose and went back to the stove to stir dinner. She said, “You really don’t want to be a doctor. Or a lawyer.”

Fuaads turned in his chair to face his mother. “I don’t.”

There was a long silence while Fuaads’ parents thought about what their son had told them. It wasn’t as if he’d come home and announced that he was quitting school to join the circus. He still wanted to pursue an education. And he would have steady work doing something he liked.

“If this is, as you say, that you can do this work with professionals and be paid, too, I have no problem with it.” She winked at her son who smiled at her.

“Me too,” said his father. “It still sounds too good to be true, but too good to pass up, as well. Thank you, Fuaads for telling us. It will take some getting used to. Our son, the plumber.”

"But there's more," Fuaads said.

His parents exchanged surprised glances.

"I have made another decision. Father, you've been looking for work for a long time. Unemployment benefits are going to run out. I have thought of a way I can help the family." Fuaads added "the family" to his sentence to lessen the effect on his father's pride.

His Dad turned up one palm of his hand as if to say, go on.

"I'd like to sign my RESP over to you both. You've paid into it for years. It's thousands of dollars now. I won't need it for my schooling, or for anything else, so you should use it to pay some bills or whatever you want. Will you do that?"[6]

Fuaads' father cleared his throat. His eyes softened and glistened. Fuaads knew his Dad. He was becoming emotional. He raised the newspaper to shield his face and grunted something inaudible.

Fuaads mother put the spoon on the stove and walked to her son, cradling his head in her hands, and kissed his forehead. "Thank you, Fuaads," she said.

---

[6] BMO RESP facts. What to do if a beneficiary doesn't end up going to school? https://www.bmo.com/main/personal/investments/resp/resp-calculator/#:~:text=The%20biggest%20benefits%20of%20an,will%20probably%20be%20quite%20low.

CHAPTER TWENTY-SIX

The students' short brick walls were a study in contrasts, sitting side-by-side with their creators on the floor next to them. Not one of the six-brick structures was anything close to perfect, but that wasn't the object of the exercise. Bob wanted his students to get a feel for the bricks, the heaviness of them, and a sense of what bricklaying would be like as a job, day after day. He hoped to instill in them an appreciation for their fellow tradespeople, one task at a time.

A couple of the projects fell apart as soon as Bob gave them a little push. One young male student thought he'd be clever and mortared his bricks together vertically. The instructions were to make a pyramid, with three on the bottom, two in the middle and one on top. Bob eyeballed the student's stack of six bricks and rolled his eyes. The kid shrugged. He was fortunate they weren't getting marked on this project.

For their first time tackling a job like this, Bob thought that overall, they did pretty well. Some of them had never mixed mortar before or held a trowel. The closest they usually got to bricks was walking past a building.

"It's clear," deduced Bob as he made his way back to the front of the classroom, "that brickwork isn't in most of your futures."

Students responded with a quick rumble of laughter.

"I don't really mean that, though. This was brand new to you. And maybe you'll want to try again and get better at it. I hope that now you can appreciate the skill that goes into doing it professionally. I'm betting you'll never look at a brick wall the same way after today."

Bob told his students they were free to go after they tidied up their workspaces. He'd dispose of the brick structures later unless they wanted to take theirs home. Only a couple of them chose to lug their little walls out as they left. Bob planned to hand-bomb the others back to his truck and return them to his shop. He simply couldn't throw out good materials.

He was closing the zipper on his briefcase when a student approached him. Brian was one of Bob's mature students taking advantage of a government retraining grant, following a layoff. He was older than Bob by a few years. He had been working as a financial advisor for one of the big banks for about twenty years when he had been told his services were no longer needed. After some time recovering from the shock and consulting with his family, Brian decided he didn't want to put himself in that position again. He researched industries and jobs that were most likely to thrive in the future and decided to pursue a trade.

"Brian. What can I do for you?"

"I hope you can answer a question or two if you have a couple of minutes."

"Sure. Fire away."

Brian looked at the ceiling as if that's where he'd find the words he needed. "You know I'm retraining. We talked about that when we introduced ourselves on day one. Anyway, here's the thing. I have a family. I can't go from something to nothing when it comes to my income. The more reality sets in, the more I'm worried about it."

"You're talking about becoming an apprentice, Brian?" Bob asked. "It's not a lot, but it's not nothing."

"I know," Brian said. "I'm just concerned that it's not enough for a guy with a mortgage and a couple of kids."

Bob nodded sympathetically. "I get it. That's a valid concern."

"Also," Brian said, "am I too old for someone to take on as an apprentice? Chances are I'd be paired with some kid who'll wonder why his uncle is following him around all day." He said the last few words with a big smile to show that he was only half-serious.

"Let me ask you this. When you applied for a grant to retrain, did you apply for living expenses, too?"

Brian looked surprised. "No, I didn't. That exists?"

Bob nodded. "It does. Now, I can't say for sure just talking to you here whether you're eligible, but it's something you should look into. Maybe your bank can give you a break on your mortgage while you get on your feet. People do that all the time. They'll appreciate that you came in ahead of any big changes, rather than waiting until you can't make your payments."

"They don't even know I was let go," Brian admitted. "I thought that if I kept up with all my payments there'd be no point in telling them."

"There is no shame in being downsized. Talk to them. You might be surprised. I'll find that living expenses grant info and email it to you. And you know, Brian, apprenticeships don't last forever and the sudden bump in salary will happen before you know it. You're still a young guy and it's worth making this short-term sacrifice for long-term gains. Tell your kids about it. Make it something you do together, as a family. Kids love being a part of big decisions. They'll probably be glad to sacrifice a few things for a while if you're all in it together."

"You think they'll give up Netflix willingly?" laughed Brian.

"I didn't say that" Bob laughed. "And as far as taking on a mature apprentice — I wouldn't hesitate. In fact, you might be even more attractive because you have life experience and you're responsible. Dependable. That checks some of the most important boxes."

"Thanks, Bob. I feel like I have options now. I just don't like saying no to my kids. Or my wife."

"No one does. But sometimes it's the kindest thing you can say. And one day, when you can finally tell them yes again, you'll enjoy it even more."

CHAPTER TWENTY-SEVEN

Knobs. Jacob hadn't given any thought to knobs and drawer pulls and handles, and now he was looking at thousands of them. If cabinet door styles had overwhelmed him, Jacob thought the endless choice of knobs might do him in.

Kitchens Kitchens Kitchens prided itself on offering clients a huge variety of options and that included the hardware. Louis Harland didn't want his customers to have to wait 8-10 weeks for custom-ordered knobs, so he kept boxes and boxes of them in stock, made of every conceivable type of material and in every possible finish, shape and size. It meant keeping more of his cash flow tied up in inventory, but it also gave him a competitive edge over companies that relied on special orders.

After poking through the hardware, Jacob moved on to tiles. Louis had asked Jacob to busy himself getting familiar with the storeroom's contents while he made some phone calls. Jacob recognized some of the tile characteristics from the time he had spent online studying cabinet paint and stain finishes, glossy, matte, etc. *So many choices*, he thought, *how does anyone ever narrow them down?* Then he noticed a huge shelving unit packed with boxes of grout mix. *Oh no.*

The anxiety he was experiencing was exciting, though. He couldn't remember ever before having a physical reaction from learning about something. Some subjects interested him more than others, but nothing had been like this. He could feel the blood pumping through his body, and he couldn't wait to get his hands on a saw.

Cool your jets, Mr. Harland had said. Jacob understood that to mean it could be a while before he got to cut or build anything. But even so, this felt right, like he was where he belonged. He had his whole life to make cabinets and furniture. What did Ms. Martin say back in high school? "Life is a journey, not a destination."

Jacob was considering the difference between light grey and medium grey grout when Louis Harland tapped on the door jamb.

"Hey, Jacob, my man. Learning about the finer points of grout, I see."

Jacob said, "Just colours for now. These two don't look that different."

"Oh, they're different once they're between the tiles. And wait until you get into sanded versus unsanded grout. Now that's exciting stuff," Louis said with heavy sarcasm.

Jacob looked at Louis blankly, unsure whether he was making a joke or if unsanded grout really existed. He made a mental note to look at the boxes more carefully, beyond just colour.

"I have a job for you."

"Oh?" said Jacob unenthusiastically, expecting to be handed a broom to sweep the shop floor, or to be given a coffee order.

"Shaker style cabinets. Know them?"

Jacob nodded, grateful that he'd spent some time researching cabinet styles. "Time spent learning is never wasted," someone once said. At that moment, he believed it.

"Big kitchen. Almost 50 cabinet doors. A couple are for the pantry, so they're huge. A couple more for the custom fridge. Dimensions are all here." Louis handed Jacob a bunch of papers. "And you're cutting the center panels. The frames are a little trickier, so we'll have one of the other guys do them this time. They're tongue and groove. All you have to do is cut the right number of plywood panels to the dimensions listed there. Think you can do it?"

"For sure," said Jacob enthusiastically. "Like, now?"

"Like, now," said Louis with a grin. "Get your gear and get to it. Be safe with that saw. Don't rush, but remember, we are on a deadline. Got it?"

"Got it," said Jacob who was already halfway out the storeroom door, ready to make a beeline for his safety gear and anticipating the sweet rumble of the table saw coming to life at his command.

CHAPTER TWENTY-EIGHT

Honestly, Madison thought the classes were kind of boring. The instructor was probably an excellent electrician, but he wasn't exactly lighting up the room as a speaker. He suffered from low wattage. Madison's imagination was almost out of electrical references to describe the man's monotonous delivery, but she wished he'd put a plug in it.

If anything, the classroom part of her apprenticeship proved to Madison that full-time in-class learning wasn't for her. She knew this stuff was important, and she jotted down formulas and figures between her doodles, but she would rather have been learning it all while on the job. However, she also reminded herself to be grateful. This term would be over in a few short weeks, and she'd be pulling on her Timberlands and heading back out on jobs with Jordan.

Madison idly sketched a house on her notepad, the same way she'd sketched houses since she was a child. A box for the house and a triangle for the roof. She was adding rectangular windows when a "Pssst!" interrupted her.

The sound was coming from a fellow student to her left. He was a round-faced man of about 25, with a shock of curly black hair on top of his head. The sides had been shaved up past the curve.

"What?" Madison stage-whispered back to him, more than a little annoyed. The instructor might not have been Mr. Personality, but she still needed to pay attention if she wanted to pass the class.

The other students offered a friendly grin. "Some of us are going across the street to the pizza place for lunch. D'ya wanna come with?"

The hard lines on Madison's face softened. This was unexpected. Madison hadn't given much thought to social activities of late. Her closest friends were mostly off to college or university. One was already married and expecting her first child. Everyone was so busy. Sometimes they got caught up on weekends, but more often than not, they didn't. Madison could feel these friendships slipping away. It made sense to her in a way. She and her high school girlfriends no longer had much in common. *My closest buddies are Jordan, who's married with kids I've never even met, and Mr. Turpin, my boss. How pathetic is that?* she thought. *Maybe it's time to make some new friends.*

"Yes," she mouthed to her classmate, whom she'd later find out, over a huge slice of Hawaiian pizza, was named Anwar. He was funny and claimed to be such a genius at electrical equations that he didn't have to pay attention in class. Like Madison, he was an apprentice. He was working with a journeyman electrician at a cereal factory.

"All the free food I can handle," Anwar boasted. "The stars and moons might be a little misshapen, sometimes the flakes are super big or super small, but they taste just as good."

Anwar and Madison were joined by fellow electricians-in-training, Axel, Jaxon, Austin, and Ben. Their collective passion for their vocations turned into non-stop chatter at the pizza shop as they compared workplaces, journeymen, and jobs. Madison didn't want to make too much of one lunch, but she felt at ease with these like-minded guys. She thought, *I've found my people.*

CHAPTER TWENTY-NINE

The college semester was several weeks in now, and Bob found himself looking forward to his classes. Teaching was a bit like volunteer work, Bob decided, having spent many days hammering and cutting wood for new homes with Habitat for Humanity. You were there to give, but you got just as much back from the experience. Teaching gave Bob a sense of his value and reminded him that he'd got a lot of knowledge along his career journey. And there was immense satisfaction in helping one of his students navigate their way through learning something that was completely unfamiliar to them.

Budgeting was a tricky topic for many in Bob's class. Bob tried to make the subject as user-friendly as possible, but some people simply found it daunting to deal with numbers. Bob could empathize. He wasn't exactly a natural math whiz, but with time and patience, he developed the ability to quickly do math in his head, a necessary skill when he was put on the spot and needed to adjust a project's budget.

In addition to mortaring bricks and being introduced to the concept of budgeting, the class had covered construction safety, and government regulations, and today, did their best to repair holes in small pieces of drywall.

Bob's chambray shirt was covered in drywall dust and his normally dark eyebrows were coated white with dust, too, after he had wiped his brow with a glove still on his hand. He was oblivious to his appearance, but he didn't look out of place. He'd earned this messy state by helping students as they used spatulas to spread drywall compound into holes he'd made in pieces of boards. Their laps held little white chips of drywall and fallen, dry blobs of filler. Most of them looked as if they'd put in a full day's work after filling a few small cracks and craters.

At the end of class, Bob felt as if he'd gotten even more than his share of good stuff from the class. He was leaving with the solution to a problem at his company, and he couldn't wait to get back and share the news.

CHAPTER THIRTY

Sunday dinners at Jacob's grandparents' house used to be routine when he was little. But as he grew up, made his own friends, and his parents divorced, the Sunday ritual suffered. Now, it was a rare but welcome occasion. Jacob rode in the back seat of his Mom's Kia Soul with his stepfather at the wheel and his mom riding shotgun. He salivated at the thought of his grandmother's pot roast and all the delicious sides.

When they pulled up, Grandpa Jake was in the garage, tinkering. The door was up and after quick hellos, Jacob's mom and stepdad went into the house, but Jacob hung out with his grandpa.

"What are you working on?" Jacob asked.

"Just puttering," said Grandpa Jake. "Wondering how I'm going to get rid of all these birdhouses. There are only so many birthdays and weddings. I'm building them faster than I can give them away."

"Why don't you sell them?" asked Jacob.

"Oh, I don't know ..." Grandpa Jake looked skeptical.

"Grandpa. They're beautiful. They're made better than anything else out there. Maybe a garden centre would take some on consignment. And I could put pictures on Instagram. People buy all kinds of stuff."

Jake considered his grandson for a moment. "You'd do this for me?"

"Sure," Jacob said enthusiastically. "It takes no time at all. I'll take some pictures with my phone, and I can put them online after dinner. And you know what else I'd like to do?"

Grandpa Jake shrugged his shoulders.

"We should do YouTube videos of you making them. That would get peoples' attention."

"Oh, videos? Oh, I don't know about being on video."

"You don't have to say anything or look at the camera. I'll shoot them on my phone and edit them. Put some music behind it, a couple of graphics, and that's it. All that shows is your hands and the wood and the saws and stuff. You're a craftsman, Grandpa. Let's do this. I already have the software and it's all free. Let me try one and see how you like it. Please?"

"Well, all right. But let's do it after dinner. If your grandma's pot roast dries out waiting for us, we'll never hear the end of it."

CHAPTER THIRTY-ONE

Kevin had never been called into the boss's office and he was worried. He didn't think his job was in jeopardy, the company was busier than ever. But it still gave him an uneasy feeling. He and Bob Turpin had an unspoken agreement based on mutual trust. Bob left Kevin alone and Kevin did his job well.

Meanwhile, Bob was vibrating with anticipation of his meeting with Kevin. He loved sharing good news.

Kevin was a few minutes early, so he grabbed a coffee from the kitchen and headed to Bob's office. Bob practically jumped out of his chair to shake Kevin's hand hello.

"So, what's up?" asked Kevin. "This is unprecedented. You've never asked to see me before." He sat opposite Bob's desk and Bob returned to his chair.

"I've never had news like this before. So, you came to me a while ago and said you were ready to lead your own team, move up, get more responsibility—"

"And more money," Kevin interrupted good-naturedly. "Let's not forget the money."

"Right. A raise, for sure. Well, I've found you an apprentice. He's taking my Introduction to Construction course at the college and he's a real go-getter. Totally stoked about apprenticing here. With you, in HVAC. What do you think?"

Kevin rose to his feet. "What do I think? I think it's fantastic, that's what I think. And there is a raise, right?"

"Yes, yes, Kevin, you'll get a raise — I promise!"

Kevin sat again. "You know, I never really thought about Tim. What will this mean for him if I'm not his partner anymore?"

"Oh, we'll have to let him go," deadpanned Bob.

The men stared at each other silently for a moment.

"Kevin, I'm kidding."

Kevin blew out a sigh of relief. "I thought you were, but that poker face of yours is hard to read."

"Tim will be on a long-term apartment project for a few months, and who knows, maybe he'll get an apprentice when that's over. He's not going anywhere."

"That's great. He's a good guy. Great to work with. I'm glad."

Bob nodded. "Now about your apprentice. His name is Brian. He's been in the working world for a while and now he's changing careers. I had him in my college class and he's smart and eager to learn. I think you will get along great."

Kevin rose and extended his hand. "Bob, you're a man of your word. Thank you. Really. I won't let you down."

"I know you won't. This is good for everybody. I'm glad it worked out."

CHAPTER THIRTY-TWO

The email notification sounded on Madison's laptop. It was from Bob Turpin and had the subject line, *A Day Off!* It had been sent to her, and a few other people she knew were also serving as apprentices, but at another company.

The email read:

> Hello, journeypersons of the future! I have an assignment for you.
>
> On Friday, you're getting the day off work. We are sending you to The Green Living Show where you'll spend the day learning and observing,
>
> (And eating and shopping — on us!).
>
> My company has joined forces with Nevin Commercial HVAC, to send all our apprentices together for this fact-finding day. You'll drive a company vehicle and spend your time learning about the future of your chosen field.
>
> We would like you to return with answers to the following questions.

What green technologies are available that we are not yet using?

What are technicians working on now to use years down the road?

How do you, or the experts you've talked to, see companies like ours making the transition to a greener way of doing business?

Jeff Nevin and I believe that the future is green. It's good for business, good for our customers, and good for the planet. And we think that you, our newest team members, are the best people to find this info and bring it back to the rest of us.

Next week, you'll join me, Jeff, and our top supervisors to update us on what you've found. That session will also be paid time off from your regular job.

Zack Rancourt, an HVAC apprentice at Nevin's, will drive because he has the most experience. But whoever emails back "shotgun" first, will get the passenger seat!

Please drop by and see me or Jeff to get your cash for the day, and to ask any questions.

Thanks, team!

Bob Turpin

Madison's fingers pecked out "shotgun" the second she finished reading the email. She hit reply all and hoped she'd acted quickly enough.

How exciting was this? Madison had never openly expressed her interest in green energy to anyone at work, but now she would be the company's point person for discovering the latest developments in the field. And she'd get to make a presentation to the higher-ups. Bob wasn't specific about how much money he planned to give her for "eating and shopping," but she hoped to have enough to pick him up a trinket, like a keychain or other small bauble. And maybe one for Jordan, too. She could hardly wait for Saturday to arrive.

Her laptop pinged again. Bob's email read, "You were first, Madison. You'll be riding up front!"

CHAPTER THIRTY-THREE

Bewildered. That's how Jacob would later describe his grandfather's reaction to the video he shot. The finished video was about a minute long, showing highlights of Grandpa Jake making one of his birdhouses. It was composed of quick clips with generic techno music in the background.

"But you only see me make one cut," complained Grandpa Jake.

"That's enough to give them the idea. They'll get it. You have to cut the wood. They don't have to see it over and over."

"But they're different cuts," said Grandpa. "And there's only one stroke of the paint brush. There's a lot more painting than that."

"I know, Grandpa," Jake said. "Think of it as art more than a how-to video. It's entertainment. Viewers will get it. Trust me."

"You think someone's going to watch that?"

"I do. And I think we'll have to do more. Oh, and you sold three birdhouses. All the ones with the little balconies on the front. Can I take them with me?"

Grandpa looked at Jacob with disbelief.

"All three of them?"

"Yup. People love the details in the balcony and the scalloped roofline. No one else is doing these, Grandpa. So, I'll get the buyers to pick them up at our house and I'll bring your money next time."

Grandpa Jake winked. "So, what's your cut?"

Jacob was taken aback. "I don't take a cut, Grandpa. This is for fun, for you."

Grandpa Jake shook his head sadly. "You have a lot to learn about business, lad. You're taking 25 percent and I won't hear of a penny less. You're doing all the work. Besides making the birdhouses."

"Thanks, Grandpa. I'll post this video tonight and let you know how it goes."

"You do that. And if HGTV calls, you're my agent. Tell them I'm just too busy making birdhouses to host my own show."

Jacob laughed. "I'll do that."

CHAPTER THIRTY-FOUR

A huge lineup formed outside the venue before the Green Living Show opened at 10 am. Madison and the other apprentices were already inside, enjoying a preview as one of the perks of having VIP tickets. Advanced entry gave them the opportunity to scope out everything that was on the show floor and chat with a few vendors ahead of the regular folk.

Their drive to the GTA had been mostly uneventful. Zack turned out to be a decent guy around Madison's age. They made intermittent small talk up front, while their fellow apprentices in the back seat listened to music via earbuds or played video games on their phones.

Now, they were on their mission to gather information and Madison was determined to find all the innovations in electrical work. The fivesome had set out individually with a promise to meet in the food court at lunchtime.

Madison's first stop was the booth of a 3D printing company. Its backlit posters boasted being able to print an entire house in one day. Madison already knew that panels and other construction materials were being 3D printed, but she was here to get the latest in electrical innovations so, she wondered, what about electrical components?

"One day, when regulations catch up," said the company's marketing manager. "Of course, we're printing prototypes all the time and working at perfecting them before we submit them to regulators. Using 3D printed electrical components isn't currently allowed, but it's our hope that once regulators see the benefits, it won't take long to approve some of these innovations."

Madison dropped by a booth where a company was touting its Power Over Ethernet — POE — lighting.

The rep told her that the concept is growing in popularity. "As more and more people want smart homes they can control from an app, we're finding a bigger appetite for POE. It takes less wiring, and therefore, less time to install. It's easier on a contractor's bottom line and better for the homeowner's budget, too, using LED lighting."

There was so much to take in. As the aisles filled with showgoers, Madison began to worry that she wouldn't see all she wanted to in one day. Realizing she'd need to get better organized, she lined up for a coffee and then spent a few minutes sipping her brew and going over the show floor map to plan her route.

By the time she met her colleagues for lunch, she had visited all but two booths marked on her map. She'd be able to take her time getting to them in the afternoon.

Madison met proponents of technologies already growing in popularity, such as on-demand hot water systems, solar rooftops and walls, and smart monitors. She talked to a developer from Sweden about testing currently underway on transparent wood;

balsa wood with its lignin, or organic polymers, chemically removed, without compromising strength, he said. Transparency apparently allowed for better energy absorption and lower energy bills. It wasn't electrical, but it was cool.

Madison was excited to discuss her findings with the other apprentices. She arrived at the food court at 11:55 am and shook her head in wonder at the various offerings. The words "meatless," "soy," "cruelty-free," and "sustainable" leapt out at her from various signs. *Where to begin,* she thought. She caught sight of Zack in a lineup and rushed over to join him. *Vegan chicken fingers it is,* she thought, simultaneously impressed by the consistency of the 'green' focus throughout the show and amused at the thought of her carnivorous father's reaction to her eating a completely meatless meal.

CHAPTER THIRTY-FIVE

The pride on Jacob's face was unmistakable. He was beaming, standing on the asphalt behind the building where a couple of the kitchen installers from the shop were loading finished, unassembled cabinets into a trailer. Cabinets that he, Jacob, had helped build. All those centre panels he had cut had been framed into shaker-style doors that would soon be fixed with hinges onto the cabinet fronts. Jacob smiled with satisfaction. *And those cabinets will be used every single day in somebody's kitchen,* he thought. *How cool is that?*

Jacob was jostled out of his happy trance by a gentle elbow in his side.

"Daydream much," teased his boss, Louis.

Jacob blushed.

"I get it, kid. It's the first stuff you've worked on for us. It's a big moment. Soon enough, it will become routine. And I know that for sure because you'll be cutting a whole bunch more today. So, get to it, kiddo."

Louis clapped Jacob on the back a couple of times and walked away.

The workers closed the trailer door and locked it as they prepared to leave for the customer's home. Jacob shoved his hands in the pockets of his loose jeans and shuffled back inside to the shop where the familiar scent of sawdust hit him with all the warmth of apple pie.

Jacob grabbed a huge, heavy piece of MDF and lugged it to the workbench. He used a tape measure and pencil to find and mark off the dimensions. The mantra, "measure twice, cut once," had served him well as he double-checked his markings. He hadn't made a mistake yet, but he wasn't foolish enough to believe one would never occur. However, he hoped to keep his errors to a minimum. Wasting wood or even less expensive MDF wouldn't make anybody happy, least of all, Louis.

While he worked, Jacob's phone pinged at intermittent, but regular intervals. He smiled as he thought about the reasons for all the notifications. They were coming in because of the attention his grandfather's birdhouses were receiving online. And because the YouTube videos they posted were getting shared and attracting comments. As he flipped the switch to turn on the table saw, Jacob thought, *I've created Instagram's oldest influencer!* He couldn't wait to give his grandpa an update.

CHAPTER THIRTY-SIX

Bob Turpin and Jeff Nevin exchanged nods during Madison's presentation on what she'd learned at the Green Living Show. Mads was the last to speak and it was obvious that she had done the most preparation. One of the other apprentices with the Nevin team had only looked at the ceiling and delivered a brief, monotone oration about bamboo flooring and composite decking. *Not everyone is cut out for public speaking,* thought Bob. *But Madison is poised and shows definite leadership qualities. I'll keep that in mind as this company continues to grow.*

Madison had hauled in a large easel and paper roll on which she wrote point-form notes with a Sharpie. Excitement and passion oozed from her voice as she offered her well-thought-out perspectives on a variety of innovations.

Her talk was winding down on the subject of worker safety.

"Robots," said Madison, "are making the job safer in places where human electrical workers can get hurt. Some electricians are using Smartwatches that can detect high voltage areas and set off an alarm to warn the worker, so they don't come in contact with them. Some companies are using drones for site examination, and that's not just for electrical work, of course. It's safer for a drone to fly over the roof of a tall building than to send people up there carrying equipment to check it out.

While drones are more common now, they're still pretty expensive. Robots and even Smartwatches still cost too much for most smaller companies to buy."

"I'll say," Bob piped in, to a smattering of laughter.

Madison nodded and continued. "But you can rent drones. Smartwatches, well, you still have to buy them. They don't cost as much when they've been used, but it's still a lot of money to outfit the whole staff. Not to mention the time it takes to get everyone connected and set up. Robots are mostly available for demo work right now. But you could still get one if you want to show off for a big client."

More laughter.

"The other thing I wanted to mention, if it isn't obvious, is that it looks like LED is here to stay. There doesn't seem to be anything coming up that's as efficient and long-lasting as LED. So, newer technologies are incorporating LED into them. Like smart homes and things like that. LED is the gold standard and the future, in one."

Madison turned toward Bob and Jeff.

"I want to thank you for sending us to the Green Living Show. I learned so much and met some great people. It got me excited about the future and how being an electrician means I can be part of plans to make the planet a better place. It was a fun day and I even got to learn that soy chicken fingers taste surprisingly good when you cover them in plum sauce. But I think I'll stick to real chicken from now on."

Her boss and colleagues applauded, and Madison gave a quick bow before returning to her seat. Bob rose, still clapping.

"Nice job, Madison. Thank you for that presentation."

Bob addressed the rest of the group.

"Thank you all for going to the show and for bringing us your research. I hope you enjoyed it, too. The construction industry is constantly changing. Regulations and laws evolve. Materials improve and sometimes they become obsolete. There's always something new to learn about how we do the things we do. I mean, 3D printing of construction materials — who could have predicted that when I was starting out? So, I hope you'll stay open to learning and improving throughout your careers and if you do, you'll find it rewarding and challenging. Thanks again, everybody. Now, who's hungry? Let's have lunch, shall we?"

CHAPTER THIRTY-SEVEN

Jacob showed his grandfather the stats on their YouTube channel. The two men were in the older man's garage, also now known as his birdhouse production facility.

"I'd call your channel 'locally viral,'" said Jacob. "And that's good because these are the people who are most likely to buy one of your birdhouses. If you ever wanted to rent a booth at Summer Fest, these people would want to come by and meet you. And then maybe they'd buy a birdhouse."

Grandpa Jake shook his head in wonder.

"These silly little videos. There isn't a car chase in any of 'em and yet people watch 'em. I don't get it, but the proof is right there, so, I guess I have to believe it."

Jacob laughed.

"Statistics don't lie, Grandpa."

"Okay then, son. What do I do next? Go out on tour? Learn to play the guitar? Hire a roadie?!"

"Just keep doing what we're doing. Make more videos, make more birdhouses. Build on what we started. It's kind of fun, isn't it?"

Grandpa Jake smiled. “It sure is. And I never would have thought of it without you, kiddo. Look at us. The young dog teaching the old dog new tricks.”

“It’s fun for me too, Grandpa. Now, what do you think of doing the next video on your biscuit joiner?”

“We can do that, but first, come see my latest avian palace.”

Jake walked with his grandfather toward the painting station which was an old wooden bench splattered with every shade imaginable from earlier projects. Grandpa Jake held up a two-storey red, green, and white birdhouse with incredible detail on the front. In addition to a white picket fence with a gate that opened, it featured a tiny rural-style mailbox and some wooden shrubbery.

“This one’s for suburban birds,” said Grandpa Jake.

“It’s incredible,” said Jacob. “It must have taken forever.”

“Oh, it wasn’t so bad. I made a simple box for the house so I could afford to spend a little more time on the details.”

Jacob nodded as he admired his grandfather’s work. One of the small green shrubs even had tiny red flowers painted on it.

“After the biscuit joiner video, let’s do one on painting and finishes, okay Grandpa?”

“Sure, lad,” said the old man.

CHAPTER THIRTY-EIGHT

It was a hot day to be up on a ladder and Madison was grateful that she was inside, shielded from the blazing sun. Jordan was working on the outside lighting of a new home while Madison double-checked the indoor lights. One hallway pot light had burned out after just a few minutes of use so she had replaced a bad junction box and strung new wiring. Now, she was putting the new pot light in place before testing it again.

She was concentrating on the job at hand, her tongue clamped between her teeth when she heard her name. The voice that said it didn't belong to Jordan. She looked down and saw her old high school classmate, Fuaads, smiling up at her.

"Hey," she said. "Just give me one sec."

She turned the light until she heard the click that told her the pot light was firmly in place before climbing down the ladder.

"Hi, Fuaads! What are you doing here?"

"Same as you," he said. "I'm working on this house. I'm a plumbing apprentice now. Just finishing up a few odds and ends before the inspector comes by, you know."

"Oh, I know," laughed Madison. "I didn't know you were becoming a plumber."

"Yes," said Fuaads. "I'm surprised as well. But my parents listened to reason and agreed that I could pursue this line of work."

"And . . . "

"And I'm loving it. It's not just about sitting in a classroom every day looking at pictures. They let me get out and do things. As soon as I learn something, I get to try it. Isn't that the best?"

Madison nodded. She felt that way too.

"Anyway," said Fuaads, "I should get back to work. It's nice to see you, Madison. I'm sure we'll meet again on other jobs, eh?"

"I'm sure we will," said Madison.

As Fuaads walked away carrying his toolbox, Madison gathered bits of wire and other odds and ends left over from her work. She took out a small brush and dustpan from her tool caddy and swept up drywall dust which she dumped into a wastebasket in the bathroom. She flicked on the pot light and smiled as it lit up. She turned it off and on a few times, and then, satisfied with its performance, picked up her tool caddy and headed for the door.

Jordan was staring intently at an outside light with one hand cradling his chin. Madison joined him and mimicked his stance. He kept a straight face as long as he could before breaking into a wide grin.

"What do you think you're doing?" he asked.

"Oh, just learning from the best. Doing what you do. I don't know what we're doing, exactly, but I thought I'd try to help."

Jordan relaxed and dropped his hand to his side.

"I can't get this light to come on. It has to be a bad sensor."

Madison said, "My Dad always says, where does the evidence lead?"

"Does your dad want to fix this light?"

"Likely not. But I do!"

"Okay, keener. Get to it then. I'll turn off the breaker for you and text you when that's done. I'll be back in a while to inspect your work.

Madison was gleeful. She pulled a Phillips screwdriver from her tool caddy and stood at the ready for Jordan's text. Her phone buzzed and she checked her messages to see that it was a text but not from Jordan. It was from Mr. Turpin.

"Mads, need your receipts from the Green Living Show ASAP. Please drop them off at the office. Lunch, parking, whatever you have. Thanks. Bob."

Madison put her screwdriver on a window ledge and thought about this for a moment. Was Mr. Turpin looking for some sort of proof that she'd been to the show? Surely her presentation was proof enough. She remembered crumpling the receipts into a pocket of her jeans and hoped they hadn't gone through the laundry yet. Madison texted back.

"Sure thing, Mr. T. Can I ask what for?"

Three dots danced on the screen for what felt to Madison like an eternity before Mr. T's response appeared.

"Opportunity for you to learn a bit about taxes here, I guess. An expenditure that's purely for work purposes is a write-off against income. Fuel for work trucks, materials for building, same thing. We look for all the legitimate expenses we can find. Thanks, Mads."

Madison put her phone in the back pocket of her jeans and thought about taxes and accounting and everything to do with math that she knew nothing about. *If I ever want to get into business for myself, and I think I do, I'd better learn this stuff,* she thought. *May as well start as soon as possible.* She made a mental note to check out business-related courses that run on evenings and weekends.

CHAPTER THIRTY-NINE

The classroom was so quiet that Bob could hear some of his students' breathing. It was final exam day and the Introduction to Construction students were concentrating on their papers with fifteen minutes left before Bob would call "time" and they'd have to hand them in.

The atmosphere was a sharp contrast to the boisterous bunch he'd shown how to repair a hole in drywall, tap in a wall anchor, join 2 by 4s at the corner, and other rudimentary, but ultimately necessary skills for construction work. The school had already asked Bob to teach the class again next semester. If he didn't, some other person would have to start from scratch again and Bob felt he'd developed a fun, interactive, and ultimately informative curriculum. He was leaning toward saying yes.

If he'd had total control and free reign, he would have loved to have the students create something for their final mark instead of writing about it. He supposed it was the journeyman in him that favoured the practical over the theoretical. He could debate theory and technique for days if he needed to, but he found there was always more satisfaction in doing something than talking about it.

Bob was never idle for long. He and Alyssa used to own a fixer-upper cottage. However, after a couple of frustrating summers, she put her foot down. Alyssa felt Bob didn't know how to strike a balance between improving the place and having fun. It seemed that every time they were there, Bob spent more precious, sunny hours on chores than on leisure activities. She'd want to go on a day trip, and he'd decide instead to rebuild the deck. Alyssa finally convinced Bob that vacations were meant for avoiding work, not finding more of it, so they sold the cottage and travelled abroad for their vacations instead. Now, it amused Alyssa when Bob didn't know she was looking and she caught him checking out an uneven floor in an Italian villa, or loose hinges on a pub door in London, England. He couldn't help himself and she admired his high standards. But she also wanted him to take occasional breaks for his own good.

Five minutes left and then all that would remain of the term was for him to mark the exams and deliver the results. This was the last in-person class. He'd email the marks to the students and then, if any of them wanted to discuss the results, he'd schedule a one-on-one meeting via Zoom. Bob didn't expect any issues with this bunch. He predicted they would all pass the course, with a couple of standouts, and a couple more who would barely squeak past the 50% mark. Bob supposed that was a good outcome, all things considered.

There was one more thing the students had to do after writing the exam and that was to fill out an assessment of Bob as an instructor. A questionnaire was attached to the exam. Bob didn't know whether the students were aware that this was part of the process or if the page would take them by surprise. He was a little uncomfortable knowing they would hand him their assessments.

Ms. Witherall assured him that the results wouldn't have a bearing on whether he could return to teach again. But there might be some valuable feedback that he could learn from. Bob decided to think of it like customer feedback. On the job, he mostly heard from customers who were unhappy about something. His class had included a lot of laughter and give-and-take conversations. Bob was fairly sure his students would offer some positive feedback as well.

CHAPTER FORTY

"All right lad," said Louis Harland to Jacob as the younger man swept wood shavings across the shop floor. "We've taken it easy on you so far. Tomorrow, wear some old jeans and a T-shirt and prepare to get dirty."

"Uh-oh," said Jacob with a smile as he leaned on the broom. "I don't like the sound of that."

"It's all part of apprenticing. Now's our chance to see what you're made of. Feeling physically fit?"

"I guess so," Jacob said.

"We'll bring the tools. Have a good breakfast, kiddo. You'll need the strength and energy."

Jacob's imagination swirled with possibilities. It almost sounded as if Mr. Harland wanted him to run around a track or do some sort of workout. But that didn't make sense. It had nothing to do with carpentry. Jacob decided he'd just have to wait and see what the morning brought.

He arrived at work early, outfitted in his steel-toed boots, an old pair of jeans, and a faded Pearl Jam T-shirt. Work gloves were tucked into his back pocket. He toted a water bottle and a couple of energy bars. Whatever the day's task was, it wouldn't wear him out if he could help it.

Liam, one of the journeymen, was next to arrive and after they exchanged hellos, he motioned for Jacob to follow him. Liam was in his late 30s, tall and muscular, with a mop of dark hair currently tamed by a Blue Jays ball cap.

Liam called back over his shoulder as they walked.

"You look like you could handle a 12 or 16-pounder. That about right?"

Jacob bit his lower lip.

"I don't know what you're talking about!"

They reached a door that Liam opened and flicked on the light in a small room. It was more of a large closet, with racks on the walls that held tools of all sizes. Sledgehammers, regular hammers, mallets, pry bars, putty knives, pliers, and screwdrivers.

"Whoa," said Jacob.

"I know, right?" said Liam. "Pick out a hammer that feels good, that you think you can swing for a few hours at a time."

Jacob's eyes widened. "To do what?"

"It's demo day, my friend. We're going to spend this day busting up old cabinets and countertops. It's great for the body and the mind. I just think of anything that's making me mad and take it out on the old kitchen. It's therapeutic, I mean it. And it's safer than road rage or yelling at your ex-wife."

Jacob pulled a long-handled sledgehammer from a rack and bounced it in his hands, figuring out whether it was too heavy or just right for the job.

Liam continued. "This is one of my favourite parts of the job. It's something most guys like to leave to the apprentices, but I say, it's a free workout and it's just fun to wreck stuff, you know? We're all just kids at heart, am I right?"

Jacob nodded as he leaned his chosen hammer against a wall.

"I didn't know this room existed."

"Well, this stuff is valuable. We have to make sure we can trust you before we show you the company jewels."

Jacob grinned, feeling like he'd just passed an initiation. It's no wonder Mr. Harland asked whether he was fit. He couldn't wait to break up some cabinetry. It was like being given a license to do something that wasn't usually acceptable. Jacob couldn't believe he was getting paid to destroy a kitchen. A dream he'd had as a six-year-old was finally coming true.

CHAPTER FORTY-ONE

Bob typed quickly on his laptop. He never did master the QUERTY keyboard with all 10 fingers. He was what they called a Christopher Columbus-style typist. He discovered a key and landed on it.

Bob was pecking out a note to his lawyer after reviewing a folder of documents he'd received. They made up the partnership agreement between Nevin Heating and Cooling and Bob's own company. Bob's signature on the documents would signal a major turning point in his professional history. Turpin General Contractors would buy Nevin Commercial HVAC and create a powerhouse organization that was well positioned to serve the needs of residential and business clients when it came to electrical, building, tear-down, plumbing, HVAC, and virtually everything else under the heading of contracting. Getting a commercial division was the key to taking Bob's company to the next level. And it was a darn sight better idea that building a commercial team from the ground up when Nevin owned most of the market share already.

Everything looked good to Bob, but he needed clarification on a couple of sentences. Lawyers, he thought. Why say 10 words when 100 will do? All of that money spent on education, and it seemed to Bob that what a lawyer really needed was a good editor.

Once the deal was done, nothing much would change on the outside of either firm. They'd keep their independence and their own names and employees. Eventually, they'd need to hire more staff, Bob and Jeff were sure of that. Internally, they'd share client lists and join forces on jobs where possible.

Both men felt strongly about not losing jobs. They'd keep their own accounting personnel, for example. Bob had no appetite for removing names from the payroll, and because he wasn't beholden to shareholders, he didn't have to. The people on staff were important to him. Some of his employees, like Alice in accounts receivable, had been with him since the beginning. She had a part in building TGC. In those early days when Bob had tough decisions to make, Alice was someone whose perspective he relied on. He bounced ideas off her all the time. She talked him down when he got angry about a business matter. Alice had been with the company as her children became adults and had children of their own. She mattered to him. Sure, he could hire someone cheaper, but that was never the way he thought about running his business. He convinced his customers that the best materials cost a little more, but they'd last longer and do what you expected of them. It was the same way with investing in people, thought Bob. Loyalty and trust went both ways. He couldn't bear the thought of treating his staff like they were numbers on a spreadsheet, and he was grateful that he'd never had to lay anyone off.

Perhaps he'd been cautious as his company grew, but he wouldn't apologize for that. He'd seen competitors come and go because they'd spent their first earnings on a shiny new truck instead of better tools or hiring another dependable employee. Bob's focus stayed on doing a better job of serving his customers. His rewards came in time. He built his reputation first. He didn't fear failure, but he did his best to avoid it. Plenty of his peers saw dollar signs when they tried his line of work. The dollars dried up quickly when they couldn't keep their promises.

There had been lean times, of course. But because he'd always taken a conservative approach to building his business, he was able to weather economic downturns and occasional periods of slower demand. He never once thought of closing up or stayed awake at night worrying about how to make payroll.

And he had enjoyed the fruits of his labours. He and Alyssa loved to travel, and their girls had been all over the world with them. They had a beautiful home and didn't have to check their bank balance before going out for a nice dinner. That was his definition of success. Looking after your family. Giving them a good life and being able to look himself in the mirror and knowing he did his best to always be honest and ethical.

He still loved the business. It wasn't always easy to step aside and let someone younger take over the labour part of the job but when the time came, Bob found he enjoyed the role of mentor. After all, he'd paid his dues and done more than his share of the heavy lifting on a job. This was a hands-on learning business and Bob felt a responsibility to grow the next generation of contractors and skilled tradespeople. The best thing he could do was get out of their way and let them learn.

And that's how he decided to accept the part-time teaching position for another term. He loved the buzz of being on campus and drew energy from the enthusiasm of his students. Teaching gave him another opportunity to help guide the future of construction. And it gave him the first pick of students who showed promise. There was no guarantee they'd want to leap into apprenticeship right away, but Bob could start the conversation. Good people with potential were hard to find and Bob was prepared to use any advantage he could find to source them. Brian was going to be one of his success stories, Bob was sure of it.

CHAPTER FORTY-TWO

Dust was everywhere. Up Jacob's nose. In his ears. Coating his hair even though he'd worn a baseball cap. He couldn't believe there could be so much dust on one job.

And it was more than dust, really. It was years' worth of dead skin cells and fingernail clippings. That's what the other guys on the kitchen demo team told Jacob, anyway, teasing the new guy. And he wasn't too pleased about that, coated in the stuff as he was, like a chicken leg covered in the Colonel's special recipe.

Not only was he dirty, but he was also tired. The kind of tired that only happens after a body has been pushed beyond what's reasonable. He felt twice his age, as muscles, he never knew he had throbbed and ached. The muscles under his arms felt like they were on fire after raising the sledgehammer hundreds of times as he brought down cupboards and broke up laminate countertops.

As exhausted and filthy as he was, Jacob knew that after a hot shower and a good night's sleep, he'd be ready to do it all again. Destroying that kitchen was some of the most fun he'd had, not just on the job, but anywhere. If learning carpentry was making a man out of him, Jacob thought that wrecking a kitchen brought out the little boy in him. In all of the guys, actually. They laughed and joked, even as they groaned with effort. That kitchen might have been ugly, but it had also been installed well and took all of their collective muscle to bring it down and out to the dumpster.

Demo day required teamwork and helped camaraderie, but it also inspired competitiveness among the employees. No one wanted to be the weak link in the chain. That helped explain why Jacob was so sore. He wasn't about to let the older, more experienced guys show him up. It was a matter of pride.

Tomorrow, they would start installing the new, custom kitchen with soft-close cupboards, a huge island with four stools, and granite countertops. But that was tomorrow. Tonight, Jacob needed to get cleaned up and rest his exhausted body.

CHAPTER FORTY-THREE

Nestled in the middle of new messages from the usual suspects — Lululemon, a few of her girlfriends and another forwarded joke from her mom — Madison's old high school principal's name leapt out at her. Mr. Mings had responded to her email about promoting the trades.

Dear Madison:

How delightful to hear from you!

As Principal, it pleases me to learn that you've found a vocation that inspires. and excites you. You were always a good student and a pleasure to interact with.

Your point about not suggesting the trades as a post-secondary possibility is well taken. There are historical reasons for this. Back in my school days, the "trade school" was suggested mainly to students who fared poorly in high school. How short-sighted and discriminatory! We have carried on that legacy, to my great embarrassment, and have not been showing our students the full array of options they have before them.

This practice shall end at once. Where would we be without our skilled tradespeople? I dare say we'd be shivering in the dark in unspeakable filth!

I have instructed our guidance counsellors to get brochures for local trade schools to display alongside those for college and university courses. They will also specifically discuss trades with students, especially those who are not already certain about their future plans.

At this high school, we are equally proud of our plumbers as we are of our doctors, and our construction workers, and our lawyers. Your happiness and fulfilment in whatever work you choose is what matters.

Thank you for bringing this oversight to my attention, Madison. Please consider it corrected!

Sincerely,
E Mings

The principal's response couldn't have been better. Madison was thrilled that her request was taken seriously and implemented so quickly. She couldn't quite believe it, actually. But instead of feeling that her task was complete, Mr. Mings' reaction compelled her to start making a list of other schools in the area. *No*, she thought, *that's small thinking.* She Googled the head of the school board. *But why stop there*, she thought, as she typed into the search field: *Minister of Education*.

CHAPTER FORTY-FOUR

Grandpa Jake always thought a birdhouse made a great gift, but it wasn't until he hit upon his big idea that the birdhouse-buying market started to agree with him — customization.

Does your uncle collect gas station memorabilia? Well, so do his birds! Jake crafted tiny replica logos and gas pumps for the house. Is your teacher into gardening? Then her birdhouse should be surrounded by the prettiest garden of all.

Jake and his grandson worked together on hockey-themed birdhouses, golfing birdhouses, and even a little artist's birdhouse with a tiny replica easel, paints, and mini-paintings all around. However, Jacob had been getting busier since he started working for Kitchens Kitchens Kitchens. He was too worn out this week to help with the houses. *It wasn't easy becoming a responsible adult*, thought Jacob.

Grandpa Jake also got a kick out of the questions he received from YouTube viewers and Facebook followers. He didn't have the patience for the intricacies of social media, so he left that up to his grandson. It seemed that every time he tried to sign into something, he'd forgotten his password. So, he narrowed his passwords down to one and that was for his email account. Jacob emailed the questions to him, he typed an answer back, and whatever happened in between was none of his concern.

He chiselled a piece of balsa wood he was shaping into a tiny Eiffel Tower. *Am I growing a fan base*, he wondered, *and do I want fans?* He mulled this over for a few minutes and decided that if fans stayed at arm's length, and they bought birdhouses, they were a good thing to have.

The sound of a car pulling into the driveway broke his concentration. It was Jacob, arriving for a rare drop-in visit.

"Hey Grandpa," Jacob called into the open garage as he exited his mom's minivan.

"Hello, lad. You're just in time."

Grandpa Jake grabbed a broom and handed it to his grandson as he entered the garage.

"Jeez, Grandpa. I'm starting to think that carpentry is 99% sweeping up!"

"You're catching on, lad."

Jacob began sweeping sawdust as his grandfather returned to his piece of balsa.

"So Grandpa," Jacob said, "birdhouse sales are slowing down. They've dropped off, actually. Not much action right now.

Jake nodded.

"It makes sense with the seasons changing and birders more likely to put out suet than buy a pretty new birdhouse that would be exposed to the elements all winter. Sales will pick up again in the spring when people start thinking about sprucing up the yard."

"I was thinking, maybe it's time to add a new style to the lineup? Stay ahead of the curve. Come out with a whole new design in the spring."

"Uh huh," Grandpa Jake said absently.

"What do birds like?" asked Jacob.

"Birdseed."

"Then why don't we put more birdseed outside, around the feeder? On little trays like vertical satellite dishes attached to the roofs?"

"Squirrels."

"Oh right," said Jacob.

Jacob leaned on his broom and chewed his lower lip, hoping to come up with an idea that would wow his grandfather.

"Superhero bird feeders! Batman. Thor. Wolverine. Spider-man."

"Copyright."

"But what are the chances that . . ."

Grandpa Jake interrupted him.

"I'd know. Even if no one else ever had a problem with us using the images. I'd know. They're not ours to take."

"Yeah," said Jacob. "I get it."

Jacob got his broom moving against the wood shavings until another idea struck him.

"What if we make them little versions of the buyer's actual house? With house numbers on them and everything? They'll take more time to build, but you can charge more. They'd be truly custom, one of a kind."

"You might have something there. I've seen that done with mailboxes. It's a little higher end than my usual builds. It would certainly be a challenge. They could be wedding gifts, housewarming gifts, or anytime someone has a little pride in their home. I like that, kid."

Jacob beamed. His grandfather continued.

"I'll build a couple over the winter. I'll start with my own house. You can help me get some photos of the birdhouse and the real thing together to show how much alike they look."

"Whoa, Grandpa, you're thinking like a marketer. Pretty soon you won't need me anymore."

"No way, son. This is a two-person operation. You're the brains and I'm the muscle. Or something like that."

Both men laughed and Jacob put the broom back to work.

CHAPTER FORTY-FIVE

"So, the family's expanding. We're having another kid. My wife is due next spring."

Jordan spoke in a matter-of-fact way as he tightened screws around an outdoor light fixture. He was talking to Madison who was up another ladder at the far side of the client's huge porch.

"Jordan!" Madison yelled excitedly. "That's how you tell someone you're having another baby? Like you've decided on a ham sub for lunch?"

Jordan laughed. "After the first one, they're a little anticlimactic."

"Oh that's great," said Madison. "This second-born kid is LOVING that tidbit of information."

Jordan laughed a little more heartily.

"Anyway, we figured this was a good time to decide whether to pick up stakes, you know? Move back east, closer to my wife's family. Our hands will be full with two kids under the age of five. We've talked about moving on and off and never really settled on whether to do it or not."

"And?"

"And we decided to stay. This is a great job with a future. We have good friends here. I'm sure her parents would like to have us closer, but this is our home. So, you're stuck with me, kiddo."

Madison tried not to show the relief she was feeling. Jordan had been instructing her from the beginning and she didn't want to have to start looking for another journeyman to apprentice under. They had a good working relationship and had developed a short-hand way of speaking, and she was glad he'd be around to see her through to her certification as an electrician.

"That's good news," Madison said evenly. "It's good that you're not going to be dragging your kids all over the country. They need stability. So I've heard."

"Thanks, Dr. Spock," said Jordan dryly. "I appreciate you sharing your wealth of parenting wisdom with me."

"Shut up," said Madison as her face reddened.

They worked in silence for a few minutes. They'd come to think of each other as siblings, though neither one of them would ever admit it. Jordan liked having Madison on the job as his "little buddy." She was part assistant, part colleague, and a source of pride for him as her skills developed. Jordan had already decided he'd like to take on another apprentice once Madison moved on. And Madison had decided she wanted to bring on an apprentice once she became a journeyman.

However, those plans hinged on finding more apprentices. The scarcity of budding tradespeople was a constant concern. Who would professionals hand the torch to when they retired?

It was a matter of perception, in Jordan's view. People had to get over their belief that higher education was the only path to success in life. Jordan's income was already close to six figures. And he didn't have the burden of student loans nagging at him.

More kids need to be like Madison, he thought. She had the confidence to stand up to her parents' biases and convince them by using facts. She wasn't afraid to launch into an uncomfortable but rational discussion about how their expectations didn't mesh with her aspirations. But even before that, she had the presence of mind to explore options outside of the narrow road her parents imagined she'd take. And now, according to Mads, they get it and they're happy for her. And just look at her go. That young woman was heading places with her career. Jordan wouldn't be surprised if one day she owned her own company and employed people like him. The thought made him smile with satisfaction as he came down his ladder and went around the back of the house to check on her earlier work.

If you'd asked Madison a year ago, she would have said she was afraid of heights. But she'd been up and down tall ladders so many times since then, with the job at hand on her mind, it barely phased her. *I wonder if distracting myself would also help me get over my fear of spiders and bees*, she thought, as a car pulled into the driveway.

It was the homeowner in a faded red Pontiac Sunfire. A neighbour had given Madison and Jordan access to the house and the electrical panel in the basement. Madison looked briefly at the car and returned her attention to installing a delicate white globe over the lightbulb. The globe was large and awkward to hold in one hand while turning a screwdriver with the other. The end of her tongue protruded between her teeth as she concentrated on not dropping the fragile glass.

"Hello there, Madison."

Madison looked down to find one of her former high school teachers, Ms. Martin, looking up. Ms. Martin was partly responsible for Madison discovering an affinity for electrical work and Madison had always hoped for an opportunity to thank her. After all, Madison had met Bob Turpin in Ms. Martin's class on Career Day. It seemed so long ago, but as she did quick math in her head, Madison concluded that it had only been about a year. She had no idea she'd been working on her former teacher's home.

"Ms. Martin," Madison said with genuine delight. The globe now firmly in place, she came down the ladder quickly and stuck out her right hand. Ms. Martin shook it.

"Well, look at you. Last I heard you were going to Bob's company to see about an apprenticeship. It looks like it worked out well."

Madison grinned.

"It did! I've been on the job and taking classes since then. I'll be going into my second year of apprenticeship soon. It's a great job. I love it."

"I'm so glad to hear that, Madison. I always knew you'd do well at whatever you put your mind to."

"Thanks, Ms. M. I appreciate you saying that."

"And by the looks of things here, I have new light fixtures all around. Just what I wanted."

"We're just about to do a final test to make sure they're all working properly."

"We?"

"Oh yes, the journeyman I work with. Jordan. He's around here somewhere."

"Great! I'd love to meet him."

Ms. Martin paused and considered Madison for a moment, causing the younger woman to look down and shuffle her feet to disturb the silence. Finally, she said, "Madison, I wonder if you'd like to do something for me. For the school."

Madison looked up. "What's that?"

"Career day. It's coming up in a couple of weeks and I'd like you to speak to my class about your experience becoming an electrician. I think they'll relate to you because you were just in their position a year ago. Deciding what to do after high school. And look at you now! Will you do it?"

Madison was flattered. She thought about how last Career Day changed the course of her life. She was introduced to a line of work and a way of life that she hadn't considered before. Bob Turpin had exposed her to the importance of skilled trades and how there would always be work for those working in them. How a lack of people going into the trades was causing backlogs for certain types of work. That it paid well and was a workable alternative to post-secondary education and its student loans and heavy debt load. She was able to start making money right away and learn skills as she did.

Bob Turpin was now her boss and he treated her like a junior colleague, not a kid. Madison had even been able to bring her parents around to accept that she wasn't going to follow the life path they had imagined for her. Maybe Madison could do that for another student who was struggling with the same concerns? Here she was, just a year out of high school, and already she had a career that could serve as an example to others.

"I'd love to do that," Madison said. "Can you send me an email about it, so I have something to show Bob when I ask for the time off?"

"Terrific! Sure, I'll email the details to you."

Madison pulled a card out of her pocket and handed it to Ms. Martin.

"Here's how you can reach me. I'll look forward to it!"

Madison was already imagining how she'd dress for the class in her steel-toed boots and wearing her tool belt. She'd probably have to come straight from work and head right back to a job anyway. There was no sense in changing her clothes. Plus, looking the part would add to the authenticity of her message. That there was more than one way to map out a successful future, and she saw herself doing so as a licensed electrician.

Ms. Martin looked at Madison's card and nodded.

"Talk to you soon, Madison. Thanks for your work today. And say hi to Bob for me."

"I will. And you're welcome," said Madison, as Jordan rounded the corner of the house and came into sight, holding a tablet in one hand and a paper printout in the other. "It was our pleasure."

"See you in a couple of weeks," said Ms. Martin as she closed her front door.

Yes, you will, thought Madison, whose mind was already whirring with possibilities.

CHAPTER FORTY-SIX

"You could retire right now. Appoint a successor. Or sell the company. Do whatever you want. You could do it if that's what you wanted to do."

The financial advisor's words took Bob and Alyssa by surprise. The three of them were sitting at the couple's kitchen table. Half-drunk cups of coffee dotted the polished oak wood along with crumbs from a half-eaten plate of cookies. The advisor, a thin, bearded man in his sixties, leaned on his elbows as he shared the good news.

Bob and Alyssa already knew they were doing well. The house was paid for, they had growing savings and investments, and no debt. Bob had opened his first RRSP while he was in his mid-twenties. At the time, his friends thought he was crazy to "waste" his meagre income on a future he couldn't even see. He'd taken solid advice and his portfolio had grown accordingly.

But retire? Now? At his age? It was unthinkable. He had almost two decades of prime working life ahead of him, if not more. Retirement wasn't even on his mind. He spent his time thinking about growing his company, not selling it to the highest bidder. He had just forged a new partnership with Nevin's company, and they hadn't yet realized the growth they expected from it. It would take a little time. He needed to nurture it, like a newly planted tree.

Bob looked at his wife with pleading eyes. Alyssa smiled at Bob warmly. As much as she might like the idea of Bob having freedom from the daily grind, and the travel and adventure it might bring, she knew her husband too well to think he'd walk away before the age of 50. What would he even do with his time? She couldn't imagine it.

"Maybe the numbers say I could retire but that's not what my heart tells me. I have a lot more work to do and things I want to do before retirement arrives. That's still a long way off."

The financial advisor pursed his lips.

"I'm just saying that you're in a position that thousands, no, millions of people would like to be in. But how you conduct your life is, of course, entirely up to you. Me? I'd be on a tropical beach under a big umbrella with a cold beer. But hey, that's me."

Alyssa said, "We're grateful to know we're in such a fortunate situation. But Bob retiring? That's not in the cards for the foresee-able future."

The advisor put his palms up in surrender.

"Okay. Okay. Well, most people would be jumping up and down at this point but, hey, you're not most people, right? I don't get to share this kind of news every day, either. It's a big kick for me, too, you know." He winked.

"Yeah," agreed Bob. "It'll take a while to sink in, but I know for sure that I don't want anything in my life to change right now. Not the big stuff, anyway. I just ... I'm so thankful for the way things have gone for us. We're very, very lucky."

The advisor shook his head.

"Not entirely, Bob. You're the captain of this ship. Your decisions along the way — both of you — that's what made the difference."

Bob and Alyssa's eyes met again, and Bob shrugged.

"I guess *we* did it then, honey," he said with a wide smile.

"It's the whole package," the advisor said. "Your education, career, living within your means, saving money, investing well. But it all starts with what you do for a living. You chose wisely. Lawyers, doctors — they can do very well, don't get me wrong. But they also spend years digging out of debt. And ask any banker. Keeping up appearances can get expensive. Not as many of them as you think is in the enviable financial position you're in right now."

"So," said Bob, "since we're clear that I have no plans to retire, what should we do? Stay the course? Or maybe find some new investments."

"That's entirely up to you," said the advisor. "I took the liberty of looking into some pretty solid ideas. Strip malls. Apartment buildings. And I have some thoughts outside of bricks and mortar. But I tend to go back to something my father used to say: Invest in real estate — they're not making any more of it!"

Bob wanted to groan out loud, but he resisted.

"Okay, let's check it out. Show us what you've got."

Bob and Alyssa leaned in closer to the file folder as the advisor began spreading papers across the table. *I am lucky*, thought Bob. *And my dad used to say, you make your own luck.*

THE AUTHORS

John Finan

As a Licensed electrician, contractor and university drop out. John has a unique perspective on being in "the trades".

Once widely considered a job you failed into, the trades of today are far from that. John considers his electrical path to be a lucky break that came at the right time and he encourages every young person looking toward a bright future to consider this path.

John has been married for over 30 years, has two children and three grandchildren and lives in London Ontario. He has built and purchased several contracting businesses that employ a wide range of trades professionals. This, he says, would not have been possible had he continued on the path of "debt-based education".

"After being kicked out of university it took me seven years to pay back my student debt, which in the 1980's was nothing compared to the burden students and parents of today face. In those seven years I was able to become a licensed electrician, get married, have our first child and purchase two rental properties. Very few of my educated friends were even close to getting the career start I had. Becoming an electrician was the first step in a career of Trading Up."

Lisa Brandt

Former radio host Lisa Brandt is now a podcaster, voice-over professional and six-time published author who works in her basement studio and is supervised by a cat named Cuddles. She's married to Derek with one adult stepdaughter and one chosen daughter, with whom Lisa was matched long ago in the Big Sisters program. If she had it to do all over again, Lisa might have chosen to become a welder or cabinetmaker.

Manufactured by Amazon.ca
Bolton, ON

34441391R00105